PRAISE FOR
DAVID BOTTOMS AND

Easter Weekend

"*EASTER WEEKEND*'s unflinching gaze into one hungry heart from America's underclass leaves us blinking not only in the new light of understanding but also in the familiar light of self-recognition. There are few writers who can fairly call themselves poet/novelists; the late Robert Penn Warren could, as can Jim Harrison, Denis Johnson, and James Dickey. . . . With the appearance of David Bottoms's *EASTER WEEKEND,* his name on this short and exclusive roster is assured."
—*Los Angeles Times Book Review*

"A high-stakes life-or-death drama firmly grounded in vivid detail. Bottoms does not take the safe or easy route. Unflinching."
—*The Philadelphia Inquirer*

"*EASTER WEEKEND* is violent and vulgar. It is also honest and convincing. . . . Mr. Bottoms sweeps us along with a direct prose style that occasionally seems to . . . rise right off the page. He knows how to get the most power out of every single word."
—*The New York Times Book Review*

"*EASTER WEEKEND* is a multifaceted gem of a book. . . . Mr. Bottoms embellishes the story with spare but effective detail and quick but intensely lyrical passages."
—*The Atlanta Journal-Constitution*

(more)

"This novel is bleak, sparse, filled with tension, and learned of life. In *EASTER WEEKEND*, Bottoms puts me in mind of three impressive novels: the excellent *Paris Trout* by Pete Dexter, the tight and truthful *Fat City* by Leonard Gardner, and, to an extent, *Wise Blood* by Flannery O'Connor."

—*The Nashville Tennessean*

"A wonderful read; controlled, thrilling, and impassioned. . . . [Bottoms'] talent is prodigious; his vision is compelling; and his voice can be as lyrical as a troubadour's and as plaintive as a gospel singer's. He's the real thing. Read *EASTER WEEKEND*. It's a first-rate thriller."

—*New Letters*

"*EASTER WEEKEND* is a novel of great suspense and terror. . . . David Bottoms has written brilliantly about the terrors of contemporary existence: the petty greeds, the sleazy small-town setting, the corruptions beneath the slick surfaces, the threats of homelessness, the nightmares of the powerless in a world where everyone grapples for power. *EASTER WEEKEND* cannot be easily forgotten."

—*America*

"Head-over-heels, nonstop action that leads to a denouement we could never have dreamed of. . . . And the tendency, be warned before you pick up this masterly novel, is to read it straight through to the end."

—*The Winston-Salem Journal*

Books by David Bottoms

Poetry

UNDER THE VULTURE-TREE
IN A U-HAUL NORTH OF DAMASCUS
SHOOTING RATS AT THE BIBB COUNTY DUMP
JAMMING WITH THE BAND AT THE VFW
(limited edition)

Fiction

EASTER WEEKEND*
ANY COLD JORDAN*

Anthology

THE MORROW ANTHOLOGY OF
YOUNGER AMERICAN POETS
(editor)

*Published by WASHINGTON SQUARE PRESS

Easter Weekend

DAVID BOTTOMS

WSP

WASHINGTON SQUARE PRESS
PUBLISHED BY POCKET BOOKS
New York   London   Toronto   Sydney   Tokyo   Singapore

for Kelly Jean Beard,
the good light

ACKNOWLEDGMENTS

The author gratefully acknowledges the generous support of the American Academy and Institute of Arts and Letters, the Ingram Merrill Foundation, the National Endowment for the Arts, and Georgia State University.

Special thanks to my editor, Daniel Max, for his invaluable insight and support. Thanks also to Steve Belew, Virginia Spencer Carr, Maria Carvainis, Luise Erdmann, Robert Hill, Linda Munson, and Jimmy Preston.

A Washington Square Press Publication of
POCKET BOOKS, a division of Simon & Schuster Inc.
1230 Avenue of the Americas, New York, NY 10020

ISBN: 0-671-73302-8

First Washington Square Press trade paperback printing December 1991

10 9 8 7 6 5 4 3 2 1

Whoever is not in his coffin and the dark grave,
let him know he has enough.

WALT WHITMAN

Easter Weekend

1

THE COCKROACH PAUSED on the corner of the table, twitched its feelers and front legs over the edge, turned, and crawled back under the lip of the plate. It was a paper plate crusted with breadcrumbs and dried barbecued beans, and the table it sat on was a sheet of plywood laid across two saw-horses. Connie tossed his magazine onto the floor, leaned back in the chair, and watched for the roach to come out onto the table. He tilted his head against his shoulder but couldn't see under the lip of the plate. Too much shadow, too small a gap between the lip and the plywood. A gust of hot wind blew through the open window and rattled the bottom of the shade. He watched the empty light socket sway a little on its cord and the shadows on the wall stretch and draw up under the rips in the gray wallpaper. The walls depressed him, the dark holes punched through the wallboard, the nails hanging in the bare studs, the pink wallpaper roses fading under all that gray. It was worse than the Airstream, which had always seemed more like a camper than a trailer, built for the road and too small to really live in. Only he hadn't been doing any traveling lately, and the trailer was rusting into itself on concrete blocks. One of these days he was going to have a big place with bright wallpaper in every room. No more dark walls for him, no more dreary walls — flowers and birds for Connie, and the brighter the better.

The roach stuck a feeler out of the shadow of the plate, and Connie held his breath and gave it a hard look. He'd been watching this one for a while, amazed at the delicate twitching of the tiny feelers — feelers and legs so thin they didn't even cast a shadow. And the way the roach seemed to want to touch everything before it walked out toward it, the way it wouldn't trust what it could only see, struck him as a real study in caution. It really wasn't such an ugly thing either. The faint yellow stripe near the head, the reddish-brown wings you could almost see through, the tiny hairy spikes along the legs, all these things gave it delicacy.

It stuck the other feeler out from under the plate, paused, then walked along the edge of the shadow, half under the lip. When it came out all the way onto the table, Connie leaned up in the chair and propped his elbows on his knees. He looked across the stack of newspapers beside the plate to the bare mattress lying on the floor in the corner of the room. The kid cut his eyes toward the wall, but Connie knew he'd been watching him. He knew he'd been watching the roach feel its way across the top of the rough plywood. That made him smile. He watched the boy for a minute, the way he kept his face to the wall as though he were trying to hide. Then the kid cut his eyes back to the table and the roach pausing beside the Pabst can. Connie studied his expression, the eyes narrowed, the mouth tight with disgust or anger. Maybe the kid thought he was going to kill it, mash it into the top of the table. Or pick it up, maybe, and throw it on him. Maybe the kid thought he wanted to see his face just before he dropped it into his hair.

"Hey, you know how old roaches are?" Connie said.

The boy didn't answer.

"I thought you been to college. You don't even know how old roaches are?" He watched him for a second and grinned. "Over three hundred million years, that's how old. Think about that. Three hundred million years, and they ain't changed much either. How 'bout that? Pretty tough bug, huh?"

The boy frowned and looked back at the wall.

"How many different kinds of roaches you think there are, huh? I mean in the whole world. How many?"

The boy didn't say anything.

"Three-goddamn-thousand. How 'bout that? And there's over fifty in the United States." Connie smiled at him, but the kid was still looking at the wall. "Most people think roaches carry shit, but they don't. You ask the bug people, the exterminators, they'll tell you they do. But they don't. They look a little nasty, so most people think they carry shit, but they don't carry nothing you can catch."

The roach ran its feelers over the edge of the newspaper and crawled into a dark fold. Connie smiled again and rocked back in his chair. The kid hadn't said anything for over an hour, hadn't asked for anything to drink, hadn't asked to go to the bathroom. Maybe he was finally getting smart? Maybe this business would be a lot easier now? Still, he wished Carl hadn't taken his clothes. Having to watch him like that was embarrassing. But whose fault was that? He looked at the greasy smear on the linoleum where the kid had thrown the plate of beans, and he felt the muscles tighten in his face.

"Hey, you know how many legs a roach has?"

The boy frowned again but didn't say anything.

"A roach is an insect, stupid. All insects got six legs. Spiders got eight legs. Insects six."

The boy clinched his jaws tight. His eyes narrowed. "What are you, some kind of insect freak?"

Connie gave the kid a long look. "No, I ain't no insect freak. I ain't no kinda freak."

"You're a freak all right," the boy said. "You just don't know it. The real freaks never know it."

As the kid returned his stare, Connie felt himself tense. "Don't call me that again. I don't like it."

"Freaks usually don't."

The roach crawled out of the fold and onto the edge of the newspaper. Connie leaned up and slowly stretched out his arm, snapped it up in his fist. It felt like a little wad of paper, a gum wrapper. Then it moved, a slight tickle in his palm. He rocked off the chair and stood up. The kid was still staring straight at him, his knees pulled up to his chest, his arms wrapped around his knees, his hands holding his feet. Connie thought he looked like some kind of animal trying to roll itself up into a ball, a possum or an armadillo, something you might see hurt on the shoulder of the road.

Connie walked around the edge of the table, and the kid hid his eyes between his knees. He stood over him for a minute, looking down at the top of his head, the narrow part where the brown roots showed under the thick platinum hair. He nudged the kid's foot with the toe of his shoe. "Hey, you wanna take a look?"

The boy didn't look up.

"Hey, goddamnit." He reached down to the floor, picked up the chain, and jerked the boy's hands away from his feet. "You wanna take a look?"

The boy looked at him hard, jerked back at the cuffs, and the chain rattled to the floor.

Connie opened his fist and showed him the cockroach. It sat in his hand for a second, twitching its feelers. Then it crawled across his palm and onto his thumb. He held it down close to the kid's face so he could see it, then he straightened up, brought it slowly to his lips, opened his mouth, and flipped it in. He chewed three times and swallowed. "You think there's something I won't do," he said, "you're bad wrong."

The boy stared straight into his eyes and didn't flinch.

"You think there's any goddamn thing Carl'll do that I won't, you got another think coming. You try any crazy shit with me again, and I'll show you how much Carl's got on me."

The boy pushed a mop of hair out of his eyes and smiled. "How's that eye feel?"

Connie tensed again. "Don't push me, goddamnit. I'm telling you the truth, I about had it with this shit."

"Looks real good. I just wondered how it felt."

Connie grabbed the handcuffs with his left hand and slapped the kid hard across the face. "Don't push me, goddamnit. I'll show you how it feels!"

The boy jerked his arms away.

"I'm telling you," Connie said. "Don't push me another goddamn inch. I had it with this shit. I really had it."

The boy got onto his knees and looked straight at him. "Maybe if you'd done that to Carl, you wouldn't have that eye."

Connie felt his face flush, his hand ball into a fist.

"Go ahead, asshole, hit me again."

Connie hit him hard. The boy fell back against the wall, and Connie leaned down over him, watching a trickle of blood run down from his nose into the corner of his mouth. He unclenched his fist and clenched it again, three or four times, trying to choke his anger.

The boy lay there for a second, then wiped his nose with his hand. "Feel better now?" he said quietly, not smiling.

Heat and the surge of adrenaline made Connie dizzy. He straightened up, took a deep breath, and leaned back against the radiator. "You don't know shit. You don't know shit, and you don't learn real fast either." He took another breath and tried to focus on the far wall. His heart was beating fast, he could feel it knocking at his ribs. He wiped the sweat off his forehead and watched the wind flutter under the shade, the edge of the newspaper rise off the table. "You want some more?"

The boy sat up and crossed his legs under him. He looked at Connie, but he didn't say anything. Then he propped his elbows on his knees and hid his face in his hands.

"I'm talking to you, goddamnit. You want some more?"

"What do you think?"

"Look at me, goddamnit! I ain't that goddamn ugly! When you got something to say to me, you look me in the face and say it!" He was trying to calm down, but he was breathing fast now, his heart pounding.

The boy turned and looked up at him. His cheek was red and his upper lip was beginning to swell. "No," he said.

"No what?"

"No, I don't want any more."

Connie fanned some air under the front of his shirt. "Then you better sit there and keep your mouth shut. I'm telling you the truth, I about had it with you and Carl both. You hear that? The both of you."

The boy slid down on the mattress and rolled toward the wall, and Connie stood there for a minute looking down at him. He wished Carl hadn't taken his clothes. He didn't like to look at him like that. His skin was too white, it didn't look healthy. And he didn't like looking at his cock, which sometimes got hard when he slept. "Carl's about had it with you, too. You know that? He usually ain't this patient. You'd be smart to keep your mouth shut. And when he tells you to do something, you better goddamn do it."

The boy only gave him a glance, then looked up and down the far wall as though he were counting the roses on the wallpaper.

"You heard me, didn't you?"

"I heard you."

Connie pulled his shirttail up and wiped the sweat off his neck, then took his comb out of his back pocket and straightened his hair. He held his breath for a second and looked around the room, trying to let his head clear. The place really depressed him — the black and gray stains taking over the walls, the dirty linoleum floor, the cobwebs on the ceiling and the window frames, the window glass caked black with grease.

It was a thousand times worse than the trailer, and it made him want to scream. Carl could just stay here tonight by himself. He was going home. Tonight he was sleeping in his own damn bed. No more of this mattress-on-the-floor business. No more pissing in a coffee can and slinging it out the goddamn window. No more freights roaring by all hours of the goddamn night. No, tonight he was going to get a shower and some real sleep. In his own goddamn bed, in his own trailer.

A wind rustled again under the window shade and brought in the stench of the paper mill. It was a sour smell, like the· smell of bad milk, and it turned his stomach. He looked at the shade blocking out the sun and thought about closing the window, but it was too hot. More than anything, he hated the heat. He couldn't breathe in the heat. And he sweated too much. He hated the way his shirt clung to his back, the way his crotch went sticky and the seat of his shorts rode up his ass. And all of that made him hate the place more. There wasn't even any power for a goddamn fan. He thought about taking a cool shower and lying down on his bed in front of the air conditioner. He thought about an ice-cold beer and a movie on TV.

He looked back over at the kid. "Listen," he said. "You think I like doing this? You think this is the kinda thing I do?"

The boy didn't say anything, only curled tighter, still facing the wall.

"Well, it ain't. This ain't the kinda thing I do." He looked at the boy's white back, his mop of platinum hair. "But I can do it. You understand that? I can do it 'cause I got a reason. I got a reason like you wouldn't believe. And there ain't nothing I won't do. Don't you forget that, sport. And I mean nothing."

"Asshole," the boy said.

"What'd you say?"

Silence. No movement.

Connie looked at him and nodded his head. "Me and Carl

about had it with you, don't you forget that. Me and Carl both about had it with you. You *and* your goddamn old lady. You know what that means?"

The boy didn't say anything else, and Connie walked across the room and stood over the two mattresses pushed against the far wall. He grabbed the closer one by the corner and dragged it under the window. The stench of the paper mill he could stand, the heat he couldn't. He figured Carl wanted to save the batteries in the radio, but he turned it on anyway. He wanted something to put him in another place. He wanted to think of something besides the kid and the heat and the filth. He ran through the dial twice before he found some music with some twang in it, then he lay down on the mattress and unbuttoned his shirt.

Connie was half asleep when a noise startled him. Carl stood in the doorway with a grocery bag in his hand. He walked in slowly, his eyebrows wrinkled toward a question. He looked first at Connie lying on his back on the mattress under the window, then over at the boy curled up on the mattress by the radiator. He nodded his head a few times, then his face hardened and the crow's-feet came out in the corners of his eyes. The radio was whining something country, a steel guitar fading into a fiddle. Connie reached over and turned it off.

Carl walked to the table, pushed the battery lantern aside, and set down the bag. He stared again at the boy, who wouldn't look at him, then turned to Connie. His mouth twisted into a slight smile, but he didn't say anything, only glanced back over his shoulder at the boy lying on his side, curled up into a tight ball. He nodded, studying the situation. "What the fuck are you doing, Connie?"

"Nothing. I ain't doing nothing."

"Well, that's for sure. That's one thing that's really for sure." Carl glared straight at Connie, but he pointed his thumb over his shoulder at the boy. "What you ain't doing is watching this goddamn kid. I'm getting five stitches in my arm and you're off somewhere in dumbass dreamland!"

"I wasn't sleeping." Connie propped up on an elbow. He lifted his hand and started to rub his eyes, but he stopped himself. He watched the expression stiffen on Carl's face. "I ain't slept a wink. I was laying here listening to the news."

Carl stepped toward him and kicked him hard on the bottom of his shoe. Pins shot all the way into Connie's knee.

"You were sound-fucking-asleep!"

"I was —"

Carl kicked him again, harder, and pointed a finger at his face. "You were sound asleep!" He stared at him for a second. "Give me any shit about it and I'll put you back to sleep."

Connie waited till the finger moved away, then he sat up. His right leg tingled from his toe to his knee, but he sat still for a minute, giving Carl a chance to cool off.

Carl, hand at his side, stood over him like a man with a pistol deciding whether to raise it and shoot, then he turned and glanced over his shoulder at the boy. "I'm surprised he didn't find that knife and cut your fucking throat."

"It's in my pocket."

"Well, then I'm surprised he didn't pick your pocket and then cut your fucking throat."

Connie threw him a hard look, a little angry now. He leaned over and rubbed his leg. "Why don't you ease up, huh? He's chained to the goddamn radiator."

"I don't give a fuck what he's chained to. He's about twice as smart as you are. For that matter, I'm surprised he didn't talk you into cutting your own goddamn throat. Shit, I can't leave you alone for a fucking minute." Carl pulled off his tie and tossed it onto the table. "Listen," he said. "I'm gonna tell you something. You ain't fucking this thing up, you understand?"

"I ain't fucking nothing up."

"I mean it. You ain't fucking this up."

"Shit, I just laid —"

"I don't wanna hear it, okay?" He pointed the finger. "I'm just telling you, that's all. You ain't fucking this up."

Connie didn't say anything. He wanted to let it pass.

Carl pulled off his jacket and draped it over the back of the chair. The whole left sleeve of his shirt had been cut away. He held up his arm and glanced down at the elbow.

Connie was a little surprised he hadn't changed shirts. It wasn't like him to walk around with a scuff on his shoe, much less a shirt with the arm ripped out, even if he was wearing a coat. Carl had always been super conscious of his good looks. And Connie was super conscious of them too, conscious of his own lack of them. Carl had made him that way. Even when he was a kid, Carl was always telling him how ugly he was, how his ears were too small, his nose too fat. And since his hair had started to thin some in the front, Connie thought even more about it all. And then there was the business about the brains. Carl thought he had all the brains too. But he was wrong about that. Okay, maybe he was right about the looks — especially now that Connie's nose had been broken — but he was wrong about the brains. He was dead wrong about that.

"So how's the arm anyway?" Connie said.

"You see the bandage, don't you?"

Connie saw it, all right. It was a neat white band of gauze just above the elbow. "Thelma do that?"

"After she put five stitches in it, she did. I thought she was putting in a fucking zipper." Carl reached into his pockets, dug out his change and his keys, and dropped them on the table. "I'll have a scar, you know that? I hate scars."

"So you'll have a little scar. Nobody'll see it."

"I'll fucking see it."

Connie let it pass. He turned, eased up the shade, and looked out the window. The black slash of a buzzard dropped into the pines. "So how's Thelma?" he said.

"Thelma's always the same."

Connie turned and looked at him. "So she is, huh? What's that supposed to mean?"

Carl pulled up the chair and sat down. "Why all the sudden concern about Thelma?"

"Thelma's all right."

"Yeah? You tell me about it." He turned the chair toward the window, propped his elbow on the table, and rocked back.

"Thelma's all right. She always was."

"You think you know something about Thelma, huh?"

Connie nodded. He stared at Carl and he didn't smile. "Well, she was always good for something to get *you* high."

"Yeah, and maybe she was the reason I needed to get high."

"Some people just don't know when they got something good."

Carl smiled. "And you do, huh? You and that little waitress, you know when you got it good, huh?"

"You're goddamn right I do."

"Well, maybe Thelma didn't think we had something good. Maybe she didn't think we had nothing. You ever think about that?"

"Maybe she just got tired of getting knocked around."

Carl's face went hard again. He let the chair back down and stared at Connie. "Don't ever say that to me again. You understand?" He glared at Connie for a second. "Not ever again, you got that?"

Connie watched the lines around Carl's eyes, the muscles in his jaws. He waited till they relaxed. "So," he said. "She still in the heart unit?"

"How do I know? She met me in the parking lot. I didn't go up to no heart unit."

"What'd you tell her?"

"I told her Tommy was looking for me and to keep her mouth shut." He looked over at the boy on the mattress, then at the table and the cans and bags on the floor. "Why don't you clean up some of this crap? This place is shitty enough as it is."

"She didn't ask you why?"

"Why does Tommy look for anybody?" He reached into the bag, pulled out a bottle of wine, and set it on the table. It was a dark green bottle with a gold seal and label. "You can have some of this if you think you can stay awake."

"What is it?"

"Wine, shithead. White Zinfandel."

"Why don't you ever buy any beer?"

"You know, there's too much of the old man in you."

"I don't drink like that."

"I ain't talking about drinking," Carl said. "I'm talking about taste. He didn't have any, and you got less."

"I like beer. There ain't nothing wrong with that."

"Beer's for truckers. You want some of this or not?" Carl took a corkscrew out of the bag, tore the seal off the bottle, and twisted the screw into the cork.

"Thelma buy that for you?" Connie said.

"You think I'm going into a liquor store in this town? Where's your fucking brain?"

"She grilled you about that arm, didn't she?"

"What do you think?"

"So what'd you tell her?"

"I told her Tommy was looking for me. What else you expect me to tell her? We didn't sit there and play twenty-fucking-questions." He popped the cork out of the bottle and tossed it onto the table. "Hey, Billy Idol, you want a glass of wine?"

The boy didn't say anything.

Carl tilted his head slightly and stared across the table at him. "Hey, did you hear me talking to you?"

The boy sat up on the mattress. His lip was puffy and slightly bruised.

"Well," Carl said. "Looks like you're not in much of a talking mood. Looks like you might've done enough talking for a while."

"Fuck you," he said.

Carl smiled. He glanced over at Connie. "You hear that? Fuck me, he says." He turned back to the kid. "That's not exactly my thing, punk. But later on tonight the mood might hit." He took a plastic cup from the bag and poured it half full of wine.

Connie stood up and stretched his legs. He pulled up his shirttail again and wiped the sweat off his neck. He itched now, his chest and his collarbone. It felt like he'd been loading hay. "He threw a plate of beans on the floor. I had to scrape it up with a piece of cardboard and wash the floor off with beer. The goddamn ants'll probably carry this place off."

Carl smiled. "They're all tough little shits these days. Just don't give him anything else to eat. Put him on the Carl Holtzclaw diet, see how he likes that." He glanced over at the kid. "Hey, Billy Idol, you been watching too many rock videos."

Connie peeled the sticky shirt away from his back, then squatted on his heels to work some blood through his legs. "How come you didn't pick up some more clothes?"

"That's another thing," Carl said. "You're gonna have to go out and get me something to wear. Tommy's got a couple of guys watching my place."

"How you know that?"

"I saw 'em, shithead. How do you think I know? I drove by in the car and saw 'em. One of 'em was Pinyon. And I don't wanna fuck with that guy. He's about one deuce short of a deck, and he don't like me either."

"They see you?"

"No. I caught 'em about a block away and turned the corner. They're just sitting out there in Pinyon's white Monte Carlo, just like a couple of thugs in a fucking movie. Sitting right out there in front of my apartment in his goddamn

Monte Carlo. Can you believe that shit? I thought Tommy had more imagination than that."

Connie buttoned up his shirt and tucked it into his jeans. "I'm going home tonight. I gotta get some rest. I'll bring you some stuff in the morning."

Carl brushed his eyebrows with the heel of his palm, then ran his fingers through his hair. He took a sip of the wine and looked over at the boy. His voice was quiet and even. "Not tonight."

"I'm going the fuck home tonight and sleep in my own goddamn bed. I had it with this shithole. Two days is my limit."

"No, not tonight."

"Fuck it, I had it with this shithole."

Carl squinted and rubbed his eyes with his hand. He looked tired suddenly, like he'd been working all day at a desk. He looked back at Connie. "Hey, what is it with you? You ain't heard a fucking thing I said? Tommy's got my place staked out. You think he ain't smart enough to have somebody watching your trailer?"

"I ain't lost no money. Tommy ain't looking for me."

"Oh yeah? Well, you're my brother, right? Maybe he figures if he can find you, he can find me?"

Connie shook his head. He glanced at the floor, then the wall, then back over at Carl. "I ain't staying here tonight. I got to get someplace cool. This shit's driving me crazy."

Carl stood up and set the cup of wine on the table. He stepped over to Connie and pressed his finger into Connie's chest. "Listen, fucker, we're in some real trouble here, and I ain't got time for any bullshit. If you want outta this in good shape, you better do what I fucking tell you." He clenched his teeth, and the muscles stood out again in his jaws. "This is one thing you're not fucking up. I'm not gonna let you fuck this up."

Connie didn't say anything.

Carl took a breath and calmed his voice. "Listen, Connie, I'm trying to take care of you. We're in some real fucking trouble. You understand that, don't you? Look over there in the corner."

"Goddamnit, Carl, I had it with this place."

Carl put his hand on Connie's shoulder. "Listen, it'll only be a few days. I'm calling his old lady again tomorrow. At most two or three days, and we'll be in good shape. Then it's any place you wanna go. You just get in the car and go." He paused for a second, the hand still firm on the shoulder. "Listen to me, fucker, all our lives we ain't had shit. We didn't have shit when the folks were alive and we ain't got shit now. And here's our chance to have something. You wanna have something, don't you?"

Connie watched the muscles flexing in his brother's jaws.

"Shit, Connie, I was there when you needed me. You remember that? I was there, pal. So maybe that was a long time ago, okay? So maybe a lotta shit's washed over the dam. But I was there, pal, when the times were tough, and nothing won't change that."

Connie jerked away. "Yeah, and I been hearing about it ever since."

"Maybe you have, asshole. But that don't change a thing. I came through, didn't I? You think I needed your shit? You think I couldn't have been off doing my own thing, getting something done for me, and not having to worry about your sorry ass?"

Connie took a breath. He looked off toward the door, but he didn't move toward it.

"Shit, Connie, you wanna live in a fucking trailer park all your goddamn life? You think Rita wants to live in a tin can with fifty other tin cans crammed right up against it? You think she wants to sit out in her yard and look at the fucking junk and the rusted-out cars?"

Carl was right. All his life he'd never had a thing.

"Shit, Connie, think about it."

Sure, Carl was right. About that, anyway. He wanted nice things. He wanted nice things just like everybody else — a nice place to live, nice clothes, a new car. But most of the things he wanted he didn't want for himself. He wanted them for Rita. He wanted to give her a future, the kind of future big money could buy. For a year or so he'd thought he could do that by letting guys punch him in the ribs and the face, but he was wrong about that. You hit a guy in the eye, he hits you in the jaw. You bloody his nose, he bruises your ribs. On the good nights you go home feeling like you ought to be going to the hospital. On the bad ones you go to the hospital feeling like it ought to be the funeral home. Fighting was nowhere. Rita hated it. And once he figured that out, he hated it too. If it wasn't the way to Rita, why take all that hurt? Now here was a chance, crazy as it was, a chance that might give them a real start. "Sure," he said. "I want something."

"Well, when you want something, Connie, you gotta go out and get it. Nobody's gonna bring it to you on a platter, pal. And here's our chance. We can get something outta this, but you gotta help me. I need you to help me, okay?"

Connie stared through the door at the dark boards of the landing. He hated that tone in Carl's voice, the half-sermon and half-scold, like a lecture from a teacher who's just dragged you into the hall.

"I said I need you to help me, okay?"

Connie nodded.

"Good," Carl said. "Now let's not have to go through this shit again. I'm tired of it."

"Yeah, sure."

Carl touched him on his cheek, just below the left eye. "I'm sorry about that. I don't like to do that shit. I hate it, I really hate it. I just get a little hot sometimes. You know that."

"Sure," Connie said. "You been hot about all your life."

"Hot to keep you outta trouble, that's all. You remember that, Connie. Hot to keep you outta trouble."

"And I guess this is keeping me outta trouble, huh?"

"And hot to keep a goddamn roof over your head and food in your goddamn belly. You think about that too. You think about that for a while."

Connie touched his cheek, trying to tell if it was swollen. It wasn't really sore. "How's my eye?"

"Fine. You can't even tell it."

"What does it look like?"

"A little scratch, that's all. You can't hardly tell it."

"I ain't gonna have a shiner, am I?"

"Not even close. Don't worry about it."

Connie looked over at the kid. He was curled up on the mattress, facing the wall. "He said it was bad."

"He was needling you. Does it hurt?"

"Naw, I slipped most of it."

"Good. I'm glad." Carl nodded at him but didn't smile. He combed his fingers through his hair. "So what you do is, you go on over to Rita's place for a little while tonight. You cool off for a while, relax, have a nice dinner. Have a couple of beers, watch some TV. But don't get drunk. Then you come on back out here and help me out. Now how does that sound?"

Connie looked again at the kid, who was curled up tight on the mattress, trying to hide himself. He was sorry he'd punched him. He ought to be able to handle himself better. Things were rough, sure, but it was a bad sign to lose control like that. It was a bad sign and he was sorry for it.

"Well, how about it?"

"Maybe."

"Good." Carl patted him on the shoulder, then reached into his back pocket and pulled out his wallet. He took out a fifty and held it out to Connie. "Listen, on your way over there, stop by the mall and get me a shirt. Sixteen, thirty-five. Can you remember that?"

"Sixteen, thirty-five."

"You want me to write that down?"

"No, I can remember."

"Good. Get a Gant, blue, with a button-down collar." He grabbed the corner of his collar and tugged it twice. "Remember that, button-down. And get a few pairs of shorts and socks and shit like that. Gray socks, Gold Cup." He folded the bill and tucked it into the pocket of Connie's shirt. "Rita got a washer and dryer?"

"They got some in the basement."

"Fine. Then how 'bout running it all through the wash? I can't wear anything till it's been washed."

Connie nodded. He pulled his pocket watch out of his jeans and opened the cover. It was nearly six-thirty. He must have slept about an hour and a half. He snapped the cover shut and tucked the watch back into his pocket. "I might not be back till pretty late."

Carl slapped him lightly again on the shoulder. "Not too late, though. I'll worry. Twelve or so."

"You don't have to worry," Connie said.

"I can't help it. Okay?"

"She don't even get off till twelve."

"You got a key to her place, don't you?"

"No."

"Then run by and get her key. She'll let you use the place. Just make something up. Tell her your TV broke. Hell, tell her you wanna wash some clothes or something."

"I guess."

Carl smiled then, "Hell, Connie, there ain't nothing to guess. Just go on and fucking do it."

"I guess so."

"Good." He pointed his finger at Connie and the smile faded. "And listen, don't go by the trailer. I ain't kidding. Tommy might just have somebody nosing around over there."

He nodded.

"I mean it now. Don't go over there. And don't go by the pool hall. Or the gym either."

"I don't go down to the gym no more. You know that." Connie took the bill from his shirt pocket and slipped it into his jeans. He glanced at Carl standing by the table, his bare arm hanging at his side, then he walked off toward the door.

"Twelve o'clock," Carl said. "And don't say anything about me. Not to Rita, not to nobody. You ain't seen me since the fight. Got that? I left the Coliseum by myself, and you ain't seen me since."

2

LATELY THE OLD MAN had begun to feel his age, first in the joints of his hands and feet, then in his knees and hips and elbows. Then out of these joints the pain backed up into his bones — a cold pain that spread slowly and wouldn't go away. It stiffened him in the morning and only faded when he lay out in the grass on the side of a hill or the slope of the riverbank and soaked in the afternoon sun. But today the pain seemed to have moved from his bones deep into his muscles, and though the afternoon was more than half over and the sun sizzled in the sky, he still felt the dull cold.

It was sleeping in the damp, he knew that. But he didn't know what to do about it. He wasn't going down to the camp. Not with Kenny gone. George was down there, sure, and you could trust George all right. But he was as black as an old tire, and when some of those others started drinking hard, they didn't like him for it. Also, you just couldn't tell how long he'd be around. Maybe you'd wake up in the middle of the night and he'd be gone, and there you were, alone with a pack of wild dogs.

He reached up to his neck and pulled the earphones back over his head. A crow came out of the pines and swooped low over the river. Or *was* it a crow? It was black, but it didn't fly like a crow. Sometimes he thought his eyes were going too.

His ears were still good. He could hear in the quiet of the night the far-off hoot of an owl, bark of a dog, the smallest wind in the trees, the slightest creak in the rusty gate of a grave plot. But sometimes he thought his eyes were going because they wanted to blur the edges of things. But maybe they weren't. Maybe they were just tired and it really was a crow. Anyway, he liked to sit here on the riverbank and look down over the tracks at the muddy water easing off under the bridge. The trees across the river were full of birds, and some days you could see a few fishermen huddled up on the far bank under the trellis, sitting on folding chairs and plastic coolers, watching their floats bob on the water, patient as Job.

He punched the button on the Walkman and voices cut in halfway through a song. *Out of Egypt I have traveled through the darkness dreary, over hills and valleys and across the desert sand.* It was a good song, the piano not too bouncy, but he wished a woman were singing it. Next time he was down at that store, he'd try to find a tape with a woman, a soft voice to put the real spirit into it, a voice you could wrap up in like a quilt and close your eyes and see good pictures of what she was singing about. Somewhere in those walls of plastic boxes he knew there must be one, a voice like that, a woman's voice. But it wasn't like you could ask the lady at the counter. It wasn't like you could ask her to climb down off that stool, to walk around those big stacks of red and white Bibles and show you where it was.

The singing trailed off and the last note of the piano died. Static blared in his ears and he turned down the volume. An organ started up, slow and deep, then violins. He turned it back up. The sweet notes trembled and deepened. *There's a land beyond the river that they call the sweet forever, and we only reach that shore by faith's decree.* The husky quartet voices singing smooth and rich. And he turned it up again, lay back on the grass of the bank. That song was one of his favorites, and he loved to close his eyes to it and watch the white doors of the chapel open up again, to walk down the concrete aisle between the rows of folding chairs, the clean-shaven men holding in their hands the red paper hymnals but not reading from them, only holding them open and singing by heart, following the wheeze of the tiny organ, the red-haired woman in front of the pulpit, following her voice, the voice that wrapped up all their voices in its softness and warmth.

Amazing the way music brought things back. Sometimes he could hardly remember his name, and now he was looking at her face as though he stood right in front of her, looking at those red curls on her forehead, dark curls the color of ripe apples, then the deep brown of her eyes, the thin wrinkles under those eyes, the tiny scratch of a scar at the corner of her mouth, watching her smile over the congregation as her right hand traced the rhythms of the song in the thick air of the chapel.

He liked watching her hand flutter like a white moth over the page of the hymnal, rising, zagging, falling. It was writing some kind of message on the air, words you could see being written but couldn't read. It spelled something invisible that touched the eyes of the congregation, lit up their faces, and came out of their mouths as song.

Lately this was the memory the gospel music brought him. Sometimes there were other pictures too — the building of roofs and the tacking down of shingles, the tractors plowing the fields, the shirtless convicts clearing the woods with axes. He remembered vividly the spark of the blade on the grind-stone, the swing jarring back through the handle. These were all from the same time, he thought, because the same music brought them back. Of course, there were other memories he could still call up, but they were from other times and needed different kinds of music.

Something rattled in the grass beside him and he opened

his eyes to the blue sky above the river. A shadow crawled over his face.

"Hey, Pop?" the man said.

It was all right. It was George, and you could trust George.

"Hey, Pop, where you been at?" He was a large black man in a dirty T-shirt and jeans. His face was wide, his eyes bright and full of life, his mouth upturned a little at the corners.

The old man switched off the tape player. "Different places, I guess. You seen Kenny?"

"No. Figured you run off after him."

The old man frowned. "He didn't run off nowhere, I guess."

"You don't know nothing about that. He run off, that's all. Hey, you got you some new music? You better quit stealing them tapes, they gonna put you in the jailhouse."

The old man gazed up at the black face.

"Come on," George said. "We gonna walk up to the Krystal."

"Go where?"

"Eat something. You eat yet?"

"No, I don't guess."

George kicked the feed sack lying on the ground beside him. "I got maybe two dollars already. We can walk on up here to the Krystal, maybe find some more on the way."

"Two dollars?"

"Right at it. I ain't counted 'em."

The old man sat up and took off the earphones. One thing about George, he was a hard worker. He didn't mind breaking a sweat, and there wasn't any meanness in him either. Only it wasn't like Kenny. Sometimes George talked a lot and couldn't tell what to say and what not to. He didn't mean any mischief in it, he just couldn't tell what not to say. Kenny could keep your secret though. You could tell Kenny anything at all, and it was just like telling it to a tree.

"Maybe you oughta put it down on the guitar?"

"I'd as soon eat."

"What is it today, Pepsi or Coke?"

"Pepsi, I reckon. Ain't been too many Coke."

The old man pushed to his feet and stood up slow. The pain in his back flared a little but eased when he straightened up. He rubbed his arms and the backs of his hands. Not too long ago, if you wanted to, you could make a decent meal pretty easy just by walking the side of the road. But it was all cans now. Nobody drank much out of bottles anymore. And you just had to get too many cans together. Nothing to be made off that. It was a whole lot easier now to walk downtown at night and lift tapes out of parked cars. If they were in good shape, you could take them down to the pawnshop on Broadway and Joel T. would give you fifty cents apiece for them. Sure, that was a little harder than it used to be too, so many people locking their cars now, but you only had to find one unlocked and you could generally get four or five dollars' worth. Only George wouldn't do that. It didn't matter that it was easy and not too risky. Or that you weren't really hurting anybody. No, that didn't matter to George. It was against the law, and he wouldn't have any dealings with it. He'd rather stand on the street corner, singing and playing for spare change. Maybe that was okay for George, but everybody couldn't sing and play music.

"You oughta put it on the guitar," the old man said again.

"Not today. I can't eat no guitar, and I ain't eat much lately. How 'bout you?"

The old man's stomach growled. "Yesterday. I eat some soup, I think, some crackers too. You been drinking?"

"Not much." George started up the long hill. "Come on. Let's eat us some burgers."

A crow cawed out of the graveyard behind him and flew over the river. The old man watched it disappear above the pines. That one was a crow, all right. He turned and saw that George had already started up the hill and into the gravestones, the bag thrown over his shoulder. A pain rolled through his stomach. Eating wasn't a bad idea.

With the sun coming at it from the west, a sharp light flared off the walls of the Krystal. The old man liked the way it lit the glass front, turned the white tiles into ivory. It was like something from an old story he couldn't quite recall, something you dream about but never expect to see. And he liked the bright cars parked around it. They were pretty, with the sun gleaming off their windshields and hoods, but they also meant a crowd. And a crowd meant good food, and that made him hungrier. He looked up the highway and down, waited on the traffic, and followed George across. From the edge of the parking lot, he could just catch the aroma of meat and onions steaming on the grill.

Coffee and hamburgers were good, but he hoped they had enough for French fries too. It was like George said, though. It depended on what kind of mood Mr. Taylor was in. If he hadn't been at the bottle and maybe had gone to church last week, he'd be feeling his charity. He'd take what they had then and give them whatever they wanted. There were still good people around, people who'd spare you something when you needed it. The trick, though, was not to take advantage of them. Too many folks just wanted to take advantage, get what they could now and never think about anybody else, never think about a future time. It wasn't hard to blame a man for tightening up if he thought you were taking advantage of him.

As they crossed the parking lot, the heat from the asphalt baked up through his shoes. But he lived for the heat. It was the best thing about Macon — the vicious summer heat, the hammering sun most people found joyless on the cooler days, torture on the rest. To him it felt good, though, especially now in the parking lot, where the trapped warmth felt like liniment seeping into the soles of his feet. How could his joints ache in weather like this? He was old, that's all. He was old and beginning to feel it.

George was moving quickly toward the side of the building. The old man stepped up his pace and followed him around to the back.

"You let me talk to him," George said. He stepped up to a white door and knocked twice. Nothing, so he knocked again, louder.

The old man shifted his weight from leg to leg and thought about the hamburgers steaming on the grill, three or four rows of thin tasty patties steaming in onions, square buns lined up behind them. They made a good picture in his head, but he hoped there was enough in George's bag for French fries too.

The door swung half open and a tall kid in a white apron stared out at them. His face was long and homely, and he had a Band-Aid covering the bridge of his nose.

"Yes sir," George said. "We looking for Mr. Taylor."

"He ain't here today."

"Ain't here?"

"That's what I said, ain't it?" The boy scrutinized the old man, then George. "He didn't come in. He's sick."

"Well," George said. "He usually take these drink bottles here and give us something to eat. He take 'em down to the Kroger, I think, and —"

"I don't know nothing about no bottles."

"Well, listen here, you could put 'em —"

"Look, them bottles is between you and him. He ain't told me nothing about 'em."

"But listen here, you —"

"No, you listen. I ain't got time for this, and I don't want no sack fulla bottles."

George put his hand on the door and pulled it toward him. "How come you treat a man like that, huh?"

"Get your hand off that door," the boy said.

"We trying to tell you something, you don't even let us say it. Mr. Taylor, he take these bottles down —"

"Get your damn hand off the door or I'll call the cops."

George dropped the hand and backed up a step. "Hey, we just trying to tell you something here. We just —"

"Look, boy, listen good. I don't want no goddamn bottles. So get on outta here, you smell like shit." The door slammed.

George stared for a few seconds at the small red letters that spelled Employees Only. He knocked again.

The old man rubbed his knuckles. The heat felt good rising up through his shoes, but the sun wasn't helping his hands. "It's okay," he said. "He don't understand, that's all."

3

IT WAS A SHADOW like the hunched back of a cat edging across the top of the dumpster, then, as Connie eased the Volkswagen down the alley, it turned into the head and shoulders of a man. Connie brightened his headlights, watched the guy squint in the glare and try to shade his eyes with his hands. The man reeled backward a little, then turned away from the light, but as Connie edged the car past him, he turned again and leaned back over the top of the dumpster.

The parking lot of the Waffle House opened at the end of the alley. Two cars and a truck were parked near the door and another car parked in the back of the lot under a street-light. That one was Rita's, a yellow '71 Plymouth Duster she'd bought at a police auction. Actually, Connie had picked it out for her. The body needed some work and the seats needed recovering, but the engine and the transmission were solid.

Connie pulled in next to it and cut the lights and ignition. He eased the door shut and glanced over his hood at the front fender of the Duster. It wasn't really so bad, but she ought to get it fixed before it rusted any more. He thought about garages for a second, then walked back toward the end of the alley. Something rattled out of the dark, then banged loud.

"Hey, you all right in there?" Connie stepped into the alley. It was like a long tunnel with no light at the end. "You all right?"

"Lid fell. That's all." The voice seemed to float up out of the dark, low and hoarse.

"You all right?"

"I didn't hurt nothing."

Connie walked toward the voice until the faint outline of a head showed above the dumpster. "What the hell you doing back here?"

"I ain't hurting nothing. I look like I'm hurting something in here? I look like it?"

Connie looked hard into the darkness. "I didn't say you was, did I? I said what you doing back here?"

The man stared at him for a minute. He was a short man, and thin, but he had broad shoulders for his size, and he wasn't stooped over. He looked old, but it was hard to tell just how old. He pulled some paper off a sandwich he was holding. "I ain't bothering you."

"I didn't say you was, buddy. I thought maybe you fell."

The old man brought the sandwich up to his face and smelled it, then he took a bite and chewed it slowly, staring out at nothing.

"Hey, you get that thing outta that goddamn dumpster? Hey, don't eat that shit."

The old man swallowed and held up the sandwich for Connie to see. "Ain't nothing outside a man that goes in him can defile him. What comes out is what defiles him."

Connie watched him take another bite of the sandwich. "Throw that shit away and let's go on in here and get something to eat."

The bum didn't say anything.

"Come on," Connie said. "Let's go."

"Ain't no money in this belt, mister. Not a dime. You think I got some money?"

"Did I ask you that? Throw that shit away and let's go on in here and get some food."

The old man sized Connie up, both hands holding his find. He stood that way for a few seconds in the dark of the alley, then dropped what was left of the sandwich and stepped away from the dumpster. "Well, okay. You want me to, I won't say no."

Connie had thought the odor belonged to the garbage, but halfway down the alley he knew it belonged to the bum too. When they stepped into the parking lot, he saw what he'd more or less expected. The guy was filthy — beard and shoulder-length hair matted and greasy, and more wrinkles than Connie had ever seen cut into one man's face. His shirt was buttoned all the way up to his neck, but it hung open in a long tear down his chest, and his jeans were caked with dirt and oil, both knees ragged. The only thing clean about him were his shoes, new white high-tops that glowed in the streetlight.

A hot wind came up off the street and blew across the parking lot. Connie walked a step or two behind the bum, watching him swing his arms from side to side, walking hard into the wind that pushed back his hair and flapped the ragged front of his shirt. When they reached the front door, the bum pulled it open and waved Connie through.

The air conditioner felt good, and Connie stood for a moment inside the door, letting the cool air work under his shirt. It was bright and clean in the Waffle House, and he liked the way the orange seats glowed under the big globed lights. All the Formica tabletops shone like polished wood, and the front of the refrigerator mirrored the room in buffed aluminum. Even the floor shone, and the whole place smelled of coffee.

Only one booth was occupied, the middle booth against the left wall — three men hunched over bacon, eggs, and waffles. One of them looked over at Connie. He chewed a few times, slowly, then swallowed. "Hey, get that rat outta here. We're trying to eat some supper."

Something shot through Connie, but he caught himself, didn't say anything, only stood there staring. When the man went back to his food, Connie walked over to the counter and picked out a stool. The old man sat down on the other side of him.

Rita came out of the back with a tray of salt and pepper shakers, eyes glowing, hair burning red under the big lights. She smiled when she saw him, but let the smile fall when she noticed the bum. "Connie, he with you?"

"Looks like it."

"Well, William won't like it if he sees him in here." She bent down and set the tray under the counter. "He had to run him off once today already."

"Where's he at?" Connie said.

"Went home to check on his dog, but he ought to be back in here any minute." She spread two menus on the counter in front of them. "Let's eat up and roll."

"When did William get a dog?"

"Yesterday. He got a puppy from the pound."

"What's he want with a dog?"

"How do I know? Got tired of living alone, I guess. A dog's about the only thing that'd put up with him."

"Hey, Rita." The man in the booth pushed a paper napkin across his mouth. "I'm trying to eat my damn supper. And I don't like to eat with rats. If I wanted to eat with rats, I'd go down to the dump."

Connie turned on the stool and sent him another glare. He was a big balding guy in a yellow golf shirt, but most of his size was fat. "Listen," Connie said, "you don't have to talk like that."

"Is that right?" the guy said. "And I don't have to eat my supper with rats neither."

"You don't watch your mouth, sport, you're liable to be eating it through your asshole."

The two other men looked up then, suddenly interested, and the fat guy across the table pointed his fork at Connie. "Don't give me any shit, friend, 'cause I ain't in the mood for it."

Rita threw her hands in the air. "Okay, boys. We can't have any trouble in here."

"We ain't starting no trouble," Connie said. "We're just trying to get something to eat."

"Come on," Rita said, "just look at him. And his clothes smell. You wanna get me fired? William'll be back in here any minute." She looked at the old man. "Why don't I fix you something good to go, and you can eat it in the parking lot?"

"We don't eat in parking lots," Connie said.

"Damn, Connie," she said, "you can't eat in here either. Not till you get him cleaned up. You're gonna get me fired."

Connie frowned at her and shook his head. Then he looked again at the man on the stool beside him. She was right. He looked like he hadn't bathed in months. And he smelled awful. But there was something else about him too, something sad and almost fragile. His hair and beard were a rusty gray that made his face look brittle. His eyes were gray too, and the wrinkles sagging under them gave him the look of a bad hangover.

Connie slapped his hand on the counter. "Come on," he said to the old man. He frowned again at Rita and slid down off the stool. The bum followed him out.

They stood outside by the phone booth while Connie stewed. He didn't know who'd pissed him off more, the guy in the golf shirt or Rita. He looked back through the window and saw her staring at them. That wasn't like her, turning them out like that. That wasn't like her at all.

Headlights and taillights moved in four lanes up and down Riverside, and Connie gazed into the crowded parking lot of the S & S Cafeteria. Maybe they'd just go over there and eat. Get serious. Who was he fooling. Not with the old man looking like that. Still, there were dozens of places on Riverside. It was all fast food and gas stations, bars and motels. But that wasn't the problem. He knew that. He just didn't like being told where he could eat and where he couldn't.

"We could've got it to go," the old man said. "We could've eat it in the parking lot."

"I don't eat in parking lots. You don't neither."

The old man ran his fingers through his beard. He studied Connie and smiled. "Hell, I don't mind."

"Listen, buddy, I don't eat outside unless I'm at a goddamn picnic." He flapped some air under his shirt. "And I don't go on no picnics when it's this fucking hot."

"I eat anywhere. I don't mind."

"Come on," Connie said.

"Where we going?"

Connie turned the corner of the building and headed across the parking lot, the old man a step or two behind him. When he got to the Volkswagen, he unlocked the door on the passenger's side.

"Where we going?" the old man said again.

"We ain't going nowhere. We're there." He pulled the front seat down, rummaged in the back through some packages, and found what he was after. He handed the shirt, still folded and pinned, to the old man. "Here, try this thing on."

"What's that?"

"It's a shirt. Belongs to my brother."

The old man turned the shirt over in his hands. "That's real nice," he said. "I like blue. It's blue, ain't it?"

"Yeah, it's blue, all right. And make sure you get all the goddamn pins out. I can't have you stabbing yourself."

He held the shirt up to the streetlight. "That's real nice. I appreciate it. You don't think your brother'll mind?"

"Carl? Naw, he's a sweet guy. He'd want you to have it. He's got tons of shirts."

The bum pulled the pins out of the shirt and tossed them

into the darkness. He unbuttoned his old shirt, slipped out of it, and let it fall to the pavement. His chest was hairless, thin and yellow in the streetlight, ribs showing all the way to his nipples. He kicked the old shirt under the car and slipped into the new one. It swallowed him, only the tips of his fingers sticking out of the sleeves.

"Roll 'em up," Connie said. "It'll be fine."

"This is real nice. I can't remember nothing nicer."

"You got a comb?"

"I don't think so. I ain't got much."

Connie nodded. "Me neither, old man."

"Well, it says not to take much, don't it? No bread, no bag, no money in your belt."

"What?"

The old man didn't say anything, only stared out into the darkness at the edge of the parking lot.

"What'd you say?" Connie said.

But the bum was off somewhere, his eyes glazed and empty, his fingers nervously rubbing the backs of his hands.

"Hey," Connie said, "you all right?"

"Nice shirt." The bum smiled at him.

Connie reached into his pocket and came out with a red comb. "Here, see what you can do with that hair."

The old man took it and smiled again. He dragged it a few times through his hair and beard, wincing as he jerked out the greasy tangles, then he wiped it on his pants and held it out to Connie. "Much obliged."

Connie looked at the comb in the bum's hand. "You keep it," he said. "I got another one."

"You sure?"

"Yeah, go ahead and keep it. I got tons of combs."

They walked back across the parking lot toward the three cars and the bright glass corner of the Waffle House. Connie was still a little angry, but he was trying to shake it. It really wasn't Rita's fault. It was the jerk in the golf shirt. He'd spooked her, and she was afraid of losing her job. Besides, he needed her apartment for a while, he needed a cool shower and a beer. Maybe a movie on TV, something to give it all a rest.

"Listen," he said. "When we get back in there, you go on in the bathroom and wash your face. I'll square it with Rita."

"Okay, I can do that. I can wash my face."

Connie turned his head and looked at the old man. "Hey, what's your name, anyhow?"

"Pop, that's what they call me. That's good enough."

"Pop what?"

He shrugged. "It don't matter. Pop's good. There's a bunch I forgot, but don't none of it matter all that much."

"Well, my name's Connie. Connie Holtzclaw."

They turned the corner of the building and Connie jerked back the glass door. As soon as they stepped in, he pointed the old man to the right and pushed him toward the men's room. No one looked up from the booth, but Rita gave them a stare from behind the counter.

Connie walked over and sat down on a stool. "He's got a clean goddamn shirt on, and he's going in the bathroom to wash his face."

"Smart guy, huh?"

"Smart enough."

Rita looked at him for a few seconds, then she checked the three men in the booth. "Okay. But you all sit here on this side. I don't need any trouble in here tonight."

"Fine with me," Connie said. "I don't wanna sit with them assholes anyhow."

She glanced again at the three men across the room. "So where'd you pick him up?"

"He was back there in the alley going through a dumpster."

"Looking for something to eat?"

"And found it too. Can you believe that?"

She nodded. "I fixed him something last week. There were

three of 'em hanging around out there, all beat up, noses bleeding."

"Who beat 'em up?"

"How would I know? Maybe they beat each other up. They were just hanging around out there on the sidewalk. William ran 'em off, but they came back. Panhandling, I suppose. Anyway, he was one of 'em. Finally, I just fixed 'em something to eat. It seemed like the best thing to do."

"Maybe that's why he came back."

"Well, I can't adopt anybody. I was afraid William might call the cops. I don't like to see people get locked up."

"Who does?" he said. "But at least they feed 'em."

"Maybe."

"Sure they do. They got to. And they don't feed 'em bad neither. They give 'em solid meals. Good food mostly. And they got a roof over their heads and a soft place to sleep. Where else they gonna find a deal like that?"

She rolled her eyes. "I don't care if they give 'em a steak and a king-size bed. I don't like to see anybody locked up in a cage. You lock animals up in cages."

"I'm just telling you it could be a hell of a lot worse. And you ain't worrying night and day about some asshole stabbing you for your shoes."

"People get killed in prison all the time."

"Bums like him don't. Not unless they piss somebody off. Besides, a city jail ain't a prison, the cops watch out for 'em."

Rita looked past him toward the door. "Well," she said. "Looks like we just talked a couple up."

Connie heard the door open behind him. Two policemen came in, one big and middle-aged, streaks of gray in his temples, the other about average and a few years younger, his hair as black and neat as his uniform. They nodded toward Connie, walked over and sat down in a booth next to the three men.

"You boys want some coffee?" Rita said.

The big cop held up two fingers. "Black."

Connie looked at Rita and raised his eyebrows. "You mind if I use your place for a little while tonight?"

"What's wrong with your place?"

"My TV's busted. There's a fight on."

"You're not taking *him* over there, are you?"

"Shit no. I ain't adopting him neither."

"Well, how am I supposed to know?" She took a pad and pencil off the register and slid them into the pocket of her apron. "I've seen you do crazier things. How do I know what to expect when you stroll in here with somebody like that?"

"I ain't asking to move in. I just wanna watch a fight."

"I don't want anybody else over there."

Connie held up his hands, then let them fall on the counter. "I ain't taking nobody else over there. Hell, I just wanna watch a goddamn prize fight. Hey, you ain't got some-body over there, do you? You ain't seeing that asshole again?"

"Don't be crazy. I just cleaned the place up, that's all. And I got my stuff out. I don't want anybody messing with it." She reached under the counter and brought up a brown leather purse.

"Well, I won't mess with it," he said. "I don't ever mess with your art stuff, do I?"

"Not much you don't. I came home one time and you had it scattered all over the place."

"That was Carl. It wasn't me."

"Well, I don't like it. That's personal stuff. And I don't ap-preciate you taking him over there. You know that." Rita took a key off a big ring of keys and laid it on the counter. "I'll be home a little after twelve. You still be there?"

"I doubt it. I got things to do. You got any beer in the fridge?"

"I don't think so." She nodded toward the restrooms. "Here he comes. You all take that far booth. I'll be over there in a minute." She stashed the purse back under the counter, picked up a coffeepot, and walked over to the policemen.

Connie turned on the stool and saw the old man standing by the door. He looked a little better, but not a lot. There was too much that just wouldn't wash away in the men's room of the Waffle House. He picked up Rita's key and put it in his pocket. He pointed toward the wall and a booth, and the old man turned and sat down.

"Well," Connie said, sliding into the seat across the table. "You look a little sharper. Look sharp, feel sharp."

"I used all the towels. You don't think she'll get mad, do you? There really wasn't all that many left."

"Forget it. They got plenty. We're the ones that pay for 'em."

"I wouldn't want her to get mad. She's a pretty nice lady. She give me a hamburger once."

"I wouldn't worry about it." Connie slid a menu in front of the old man. "Give it a close look, buddy. Anything you want."

The old man picked it up, and in the good light Connie noticed the backs of his hands. Between the first and middle knuckles of his right hand someone had tattooed the word LOVE, one blue letter on the back of each finger. On the left, it was HATE. The letters were crude and faded. He'd seen that somewhere before, but he decided not to ask.

"I think I'd like another one of them hamburgers." The old man scratched his beard and stared down at the menu. He read the left side, then the right. He flipped it over and looked at the back. "Or a couple of 'em, maybe, if that'd be okay."

"How 'bout some French fries?"

"Sure."

Then it came to Connie, and he pointed to the old bum's hands. "Bruce Springsteen."

"What?"

"Bruce Springsteen, rock 'n' roll singer. He's got a song about them tattoos."

The old man turned his hands over and looked at his fingers. "I don't hear much rock 'n' roll."

"Me neither," Connie said. "Rita, she does."

"Yeah, I remember them. Got 'em from a guy a long time ago. He had some just like it, I think. He seen it in a movie or something. Bunch of us got 'em all at the same time. I don't watch no movies neither."

The three men in the booth stood up and dropped a few bills onto the table. The fat one in the yellow shirt looked over toward Connie and the old man, then pulled another bill from his wallet and dropped it beside his plate. "Here's a little extra, Rita. Get the place sprayed."

Connie studied him as he walked by the counter for a toothpick, but he didn't say anything. He didn't need to start anything with two cops in the place, not with everything going on with Carl.

When the three men got to the door, the guy in the yellow golf shirt smiled. "See you later, rat boy."

Connie took a breath, trying to check his anger. "Count on it, sport. Me and you."

The fat guy stopped and turned, his lips tightening around the toothpick. He tugged at the front of his belt, walked over to the booth, and tapped his finger on the edge of the table. "You think that scares me, neighbor? You really think that scares me? I know who you are, I seen you fight. Trust me, it don't scare me."

Connie looked at the diamond signet ring choking the man's little finger, the black hair climbing up to his knuckles. "I ain't much concerned, mister. Maybe you ain't got sense enough to be scared."

"I seen you fight that Hugo kid in the Coliseum. He busted your fucking face. You was a *bum* in the ring." He frowned at Connie, then he pointed at the old man. "You see that? That's what you was in the ring, asshole. And that's what you are now."

Connie felt himself flush. He glanced at the old man,

whose face was as white as milk, then clenched his jaws and stared back at the face nodding above the yellow shirt. "Mister, I ain't done nothing to you. And I don't know what your problem is. But somebody's liable to be carrying your fat butt outta here. I don't care if there's two cops over there or not."

"Tough talk, punk."

Connie looked past the man to the other side of the room. The cops were watching them now, waiting for it to start. Rita stood beside them, holding a pad and a pencil. There was a familiar look on her face, an expression of distress moving toward genuine fear. Connie clenched his jaws tighter and took a breath, then reached behind the napkin holder for another menu and opened it in front of him.

"That's what I thought," the fat man said. He rocked back on his heels. "Big words from the tough guy."

"Come on, Bill," one of the others said from the door. "Let's get outta here before he talks you to death."

The guy rapped his knuckle on the table.

Connie ignored him, buried himself in the breakfast specials.

The fat man gave him one last look. He took the toothpick out of his mouth and dropped it onto Connie's menu. "Asshole," he said, then turned and headed for the door.

Connie shook the toothpick into the ashtray and watched them walk to their truck, a black Chevy Blazer. It had a sharp dent in the front bumper and a Confederate flag decal in the lower right corner of the windshield. He watched them back out of the parking space and pull onto Riverside. He stared until their taillights disappeared in the traffic.

"You been in fights?" the old bum said.

"A few. I was a welterweight."

"I been in fights too." The old man hooked a finger into the corner of his mouth, pulled back his upper lip, and showed his bare gum. "I didn't much like it."

"Me neither. I didn't much like it neither. So I guess we got something in common."

Rita walked over and flipped a page on her order pad. "Thanks for not starting it," she said, a little shaky. "I thought you'd punch him for sure."

"He ain't worth it."

She looked at the old man. "What's it gonna be, mister?"

"His name's Pop," Connie said. "Pop, this is Rita."

"Pleased to meet you," the old man said.

She scratched the pencil across the top of the pad, her hand still trembling slightly. "So what's it gonna be?"

"I'd like me one of them hamburgers like you fixed before."

"Two of 'em," Connie said. "Two for him and two for me. All the way. And a couple of hash browns." He looked at the old man. "You want hash browns or French fries."

"Hash browns is good. Coffee's good too, black. Or milk."

"Bring us two coffees and a glass of milk."

She brushed her hair off her forehead, wrote it down on her pad, and walked back to the counter.

The old man looked even smaller now, framed by the orange plastic seat. Connie leaned toward him. "Where you from, pal?"

"Lots of places. I don't know." He took a napkin from the holder and unfolded it in his lap. "I don't wanna make no mess. You tell me if I'm making a mess. I wanna do this right."

"You ain't making a mess." Connie smiled at him. "You got any people anywhere? You got a wife?" He looked into the old bum's eyes. There was pain there, but also something else. An openness, a gratitude, maybe.

The old man shook his head. "I might have, maybe, long time ago. I can't remember much."

"Brother and sisters?"

"Well," the bum said, "who does the will of God's my brothers and sisters. Ain't that what they say?"

"I don't know about that, but I got a brother, Carl. He mostly does what he wants to. That's his new shirt you got on."

"That's right. But he don't mind, you said so."

"I ain't got nobody else. My folks are dead."

"My folks too, I reckon," the old man said. "But I don't remember 'em. I know I had some though."

Connie smiled again. "I remember mine good enough. My daddy was a drunk. He killed my mama in a car wreck."

The bum shook his head. "That's too bad. I used to be bad to drink too. It ain't no good for you."

Connie watched the lines deepen in the old man's face. "Wasn't much good for him, that's for sure, or nobody around him."

"Clouds you up too much."

"I don't worry about it though. I ain't the only one it ever happened to. I got this buddy, Jeff Willett, he's a trainer. His old man's a real bad drunk. Can't do nothing for himself. Can't fix a meal. Can't even boil an egg. Got shot up in the war, so he gets a government check. Spends it all on the booze. In a lotta ways that's worse."

The old man folded his hands on the table. "What war's that?"

"World War Two, I guess. Got shot up somewhere in Italy."

"I was in that war." He nodded slowly and rubbed his knuckles. "On this boat that went all over these islands. I remember some of that real good. These islands wasn't nothing but jungles, jungles all over 'em." He tilted his head a little to one side, then looked back at Connie. "He takes care of him, huh?"

"Jeff? Sure he does. A guy oughta take care of his folks. But there ain't no sense in that kinda drinking. And Jeff, hell, he works all the time, and he ain't got nobody to help him."

"But you got you a brother." The old man cracked his knuckles. "And brothers is good to have, ain't they?"

"Yeah, he just about raised me." Connie propped his elbows on the table and thought about that. "Carl's a little crazy sometimes, but he took care of me. Out in Montana they tried to put me in this foster home. Carl wouldn't have it. He snatched me up. That's when we come down here. Well, we went to Atlanta first, but that wasn't for long." He thought about Carl standing over him in the lodge, what he'd said about not fucking this up. No, he wasn't going to do that. And then he thought about the boy, about hitting him, and it made a sickness turn in his stomach. How could he have lost control like that? And to hit a kid whose hands were cuffed, a kid who didn't weigh a hundred and twenty pounds soaking wet. It was awful. It was like hitting a woman.

"Montana?" the old man said. "I think I been there." Then a sadness came over his face. He pulled at his beard. "Brothers is good to have, all right. That's why it's one of the signs."

Rita came over with two coffee cups and a pot of coffee. She set the cups on the table and poured, then she walked back to the counter and brought the glass of milk.

"What signs you talking about, buddy?"

The old man picked up the glass and drank the milk down in three long swallows. He wiped his mouth carefully with the napkin. "I ain't got none on me, do I?"

Connie shook his head. "What signs you talking about?"

The old man's eyes went distant again. "I don't know. It's a lot I don't remember. Brother'll deliver up brother, ain't that it?" He picked up his coffee cup and took a sip. "Hot coffee. Good though."

Connie watched him blowing into the cup. "Hey, you used to be some kinda preacher or something?"

"Naw, I ain't no preacher. But I used to be a lotta things. Most of it I don't remember. Don't much matter."

"Yeah? What kinda things?"

"Who knows. I been to all over."

Connie took a sip of his coffee. He could smell the hamburgers sizzling on the grill. If they made him this hungry, he could imagine what they must be doing to the bum. "So where you live?"

"Here and there."

"Yeah? Well, where you sleep?"

"I slept down by the river last night. Down in the cemetery. It's real restful down there with the river going by. There's six or seven others got a little place on down by the tracks. I don't hang out with them, though."

"Rose Hill?"

"I don't know. I guess. Whatever's the one down there by the river."

Rita took two plates of burgers and fries to the booth where the cops were sitting, then she hurried back and flipped the burgers on the grill. The smell of beef had completely filled the place, a thick, juicy aroma.

"Any time now," Connie said. "William, the manager, he ran off and left her by herself. Got him a dog yesterday, went home to feed it."

"I like dogs," the old man said. "I had me a good dog one time. Dogs is good company."

"Yeah? What kind was it?"

"I don't know. Just a big white dog. Smart though. Got run over by a car, I think."

Connie thought of Montana and the two German Shepherds his father had brought home to watch the garage and the junkyard beside their house. He remembered the sign his father hung on the chain-link fence. Big black letters you could read all the way from the road: BEWARE: BAD DOGS, MEAN KIDS, GROUCHY WIFE. But it wasn't true, not all of it, anyway. Not the part about the wife. All that shouting in the house, and she never raised her voice. The kids, maybe, were another thing. But then, Connie didn't guess he was any meaner than most other kids. Still, there was Carl. And he nearly justified the whole sign. Maybe Carl figured that having a brother around was cheating him out of something. He was ten years older, so maybe he'd gotten used to being an only child. Connie really didn't know. He only knew that Carl was always trying to punish him for something, for being alive, it seemed like. And it never was much better with the folks. Maybe Carl had wanted to punish them, too, for having another kid, for bringing a stranger into the family.

"No, he didn't," the old man said. "A man shot him. That's what it was, a man shot him for getting into something. It was this other dog got run over by the car."

"What other dog's that?" Connie said.

The old man looked puzzled for a second. "This other dog. Bird dog. I don't know, don't matter."

When Rita brought the hamburgers, they ate without talking. The old man took careful bites and wiped his mouth after each sip of coffee. Connie enjoyed the way he chewed, slow and deliberate on the right side of his mouth, and the way the wrinkles under his eyes moved like ripples on a pond. He guessed the old guy must be missing more teeth than he showed. But he got it down, and he enjoyed it. Connie was glad he had done that for him. Bite by bite, the second burger followed.

Rita came by and poured more coffee. The old man leaned down and blew over his cup.

"Y'all okay?" she said. "Anything else?"

"How 'bout it?" Connie asked him.

The old man shook his head.

Connie looked up at Rita. "Nope, we'll just finish the coffee."

She figured up the check and laid it on the table, then she walked over to the register to ring out the policemen.

The big cop said something to her and nodded toward Connie and the bum. Connie couldn't hear what it was but it made him a little nervous. He didn't like cops talking about him. He sat up in his seat and took a sip of his coffee. Out of the corner of his eye he caught the cop walking toward the booth.

"You're Connie Holtzclaw, ain't you?"

Connie turned. "So?"

The cop coughed into his fist, then cleared his throat. "So I just wondered, that's all."

Connie took a sip of his coffee. "Sure, that's my name."

"Seen your brother lately, Connie?"

"Carl?"

"He's your brother, ain't he? You ain't got another one, do you?"

The cop was about fifty or so. His nose leaned a little to one side like it had been broken, and he had a gray five o'clock shadow. Connie studied his face, his cool blue eyes. "Naw, I ain't seen him in a while."

"How long's a while?"

"This here's his shirt," the old man said. "It's a nice one, ain't it? He don't mind though, he's got tons of 'em."

The cop looked at the old man and grinned. "That's right, dad. It's a real nice one." He looked back down at Connie and the grin faded. "How long's a while, kid? Yesterday? Today?"

"I ain't seen him in a week or so. We went down to the Hagler fight, big screen down at the Coliseum. I ain't seen him since then."

The cop picked at his thumbnail. "Where'd the shirt come from?"

"Had it in my car."

"That's right," the old man said. "I seen him get it right out of the back seat. He had a bunch of stuff back there."

The cop turned back to Connie. "Carl usually keep his clothes in the back of your car?"

"It was a present," Connie said. "Only I ain't seen him lately to give it to him."

The cop raised his eyebrows and nodded. "You see your

brother," he said, "you give him a message. You tell him Tommy's looking for him."

"Tommy who?"

"Don't give me any shit, kid. I'm trying to do your brother a favor. You tell him to give Tommy a call real quick. Make everything a lot easier in the long run."

Connie took another sip of his coffee. He looked up at the cop. "I ain't planning on seeing him no time soon."

The cop nodded. He sucked a tooth, glanced at the old man, then stared at Connie. "Ain't you on parole?"

"I might be."

"Burglary or something like that, wasn't it?"

Connie frowned. He could feel himself tensing. "Could be."

"Anybody on parole don't need to get run in. You know that? If I was on parole, I wouldn't wanna get picked up for nothing. A kid on parole might just get sent away for a while."

"I ain't doing nothing to get run in for."

The cop shot a slight smile at his partner standing at the register, then turned back toward Connie. "Listen, I ain't trying to be tough, but sometimes a wiseass don't have to do nothing. You hear what I'm saying? Sometimes things just happen. Some guys just got shit for luck." He ran his thumbs under his service belt. "You give Carl the message. Tommy ain't too pissed off yet, he's still willing to work things out."

The cop nodded to his partner and headed for the door. Connie watched them push through and disappear into the parking lot, then he finished his coffee in a long gulp.

After a moment the old man said, "You been locked up?"

Connie saw something different in the bum's expression now. In his eyes there was a softness, not an emptiness. "Once," he said.

"I been locked up lots of times. I don't mind. It's a roof and a hot meal. What'd you get locked up for?"

"They said I took some money."

The old man took a slow sip of his coffee. "Who from?"

"Some woman in south Macon. I used to go around to people's houses, spray for bugs. Some woman said I took some money from her, took it out of her pocketbook."

The old man tugged again at his beard. "How come she say that?"

Connie thought for a second. Why lie to a bum? "'Cause I took it."

"It's generally got to do with money, don't it. I ain't got no money, don't much like it. Too much of a temptation."

Connie smiled. "You don't like money, huh?"

"Not much. I like what it buys, all right. Just don't like what it does. Makes folks mean. They want too much or they get too much, and it makes 'em do things. I seen people do awful things for money. Things they wouldn't even think about doing for no other reason. I don't much like it. It sours 'em, makes 'em mean."

"Well, I like it a lot."

"Most do. It's the human heart."

"Human heart?"

"That's it. Outta the human heart comes the evil thoughts, the fornications, thefts, murders. I forget what all else. Nothing good though."

"Well, I ain't never murdered nobody, pal. But I admit I thought about it once or twice."

"Who ain't?"

Connie reached into his back pocket and pulled out his wallet. He flipped the check over and laid two bills on top of it.

"I'm obliged," the old man said.

Connie gave him a look. He took a ten out of his wallet and pushed it across the table. "You take this, okay? I don't care if you like it or not."

"I'm obliged already."

"You take it. And don't spend it on the booze."

"Booze ain't no good for you," the old man said. "Booze

ain't no good at all. Clouds you up. Clouded me up a long time ago. I can't remember nothing no more. Don't have nothing to do with it now. Nothing at all."

Rita started wiping off the table where the cops had been. She had a good pair of legs, and Connie liked what the uniform did for her when she bent over. Thinking about anybody else seeing her that way made him ache. He knew they did, though. He knew what every guy who came in the place dreamed about. Then he thought of the kid lying naked on the mattress, his little sausage of a cock standing straight up. What was he dreaming about? It was too much. He wished Carl would give him back his clothes. "Good for you," he said. "Too much of anything'll cloud you up. Where you headed for tonight?"

"Back to the graveyard, I reckon."

"You got someplace down there outta the weather?"

"I got me a place. Good place. Them others is down on the tracks by the river. They get a little rowdy sometimes. I don't like it when they get too rowdy, so I got me a place of my own."

"What others is that?"

"Hobos. They come in and out on them freights. But I got my own place. Kenny showed me where it was. He come in on the freights too, but he's gone now. Them others, they killed him and throwed him in the river. Don't nobody know about my place now but me. They done killed Kenny."

"Killed him?"

"Knocked him in the head, I think. Kenny, he had him some money and he had a gold watch too, a pocket watch, belonged to his daddy. Some of them others down there's pretty bad to get rowdy. I got some stuff, but I ain't got no watch." The old man rubbed his fingers and the backs of his hands.

"What you want a watch for?"

"I don't want no watch. A watch won't tell you nothing

worth knowing. I got me some other stuff though. I do all right. Got me a flashlight and a lantern. Got me one of them bedrolls. You know, the kind you get in and zip it up. Sleeping bag, I guess. Man give it to me the other day. Got him a store downtown that's fulla that stuff. Give me these shoes, too. I do all right. I might not look like it, but I do all right."

"What store was that?"

"I don't know. Downtown. He seen me walking down the street, feet poking outta my shoes. Took me right on in that store and give me these ones I got on. I reckon I thanked him pretty good 'cause that's when he give me the sleeping bag."

"Some people are all right," Connie said.

"Sometimes they are, sometimes they ain't. It's a mix. I seen a bunch of 'em, and it's a real mix." The old man drank the last of his coffee and wiped his beard. "And that's the problem, ain't it?" He wadded his napkin and dropped it on his plate.

"What's that?"

"The problem with folks. You gotta trust somebody, don't you? I mean, if you can't trust nobody, then what's the use? You take Kenny. I thought I could trust Kenny, and then he went off and got hisself killed."

"How you know they killed him?"

"I know things. I got ways."

"Well, you just gotta be careful, that's all. You can't take no chances with people. Better safe than sorry."

The old man nodded and looked down at his cup. "I reckon. And sometimes that ain't nearly enough. You can't trust nobody, then what's the use in anything?"

"I'm going your way," Connie said. "I'll give you a lift."

4

THEY STOOD by the wrought-iron fence and looked down past the trees over the dark hills sloping toward the river, rolling hills shining dull with white marble catching the first of the moon — marble tablets and crosses, angels with broad wings, huge gray mausoleums, brick-walled terraces of granite and marble grave slabs. The old man had not wanted to use the main entrance of Rose Hill Cemetery, so Connie had parked the car across the street at a closed Shell station. Sometimes a patrol car would drive by and slow down past that entrance, and sometimes it might even drive through, and the old man didn't want to be seen going in or out. It didn't happen often, he said, but sometimes. And he didn't want to take the chance.

In what moonlight shone on the front of the gate, Connie could read OAK RIDGE 1840. It was a huge, cream-colored brick wall with three entrances built into it, two smaller ones on either side of a large one wide enough for a carriage path. There was a strange, uncomforting beauty about it that Connie couldn't quite explain, the same beauty the darkness brought to everything he saw — the huge marble mausoleum with E. ELKIN carved on the front, its blue stained-glass windows covered with bars, the charcoal trees backing away toward the road, even the old man leaning over the fence — all the imperfections somehow darkened away.

Standing there, gazing out over the cemetery, the old man looked proud of what he saw, as though coming to it was coming to something of his own making, or at least his own discovery. He scanned the rows of tombstones and the narrow, concrete carriage paths winding around the hills, and Connie thought of the battlefields of Montana, of standing with his father and staring down the falling ridges toward the Little Bighorn River. He studied the old man as he turned his head slowly from side to side, taking in the whole graveyard. On his face was an expression of cautious fascination. Maybe that was what it felt like to gaze down into that valley at the river and the trees and the endless lodges of the Sioux.

"Hey, you know who Custer was?"

The old man's stare wandered out among the stones. "I heard of him."

"I went to his grave once."

"Where's that?"

"Montana."

"I been there, I think."

"Yeah? When was that?"

"Who knows. I been everywhere once." The old man turned and glanced at Connie. He stared back out over the cemetery. "That Mr. Custer," he said, "he wasn't too smart, I guess."

Connie followed the old man's gaze into the middle of the graveyard, where the hills broke into terraces of stone. "Oh yeah? How come?"

"Should've minded his own business. Left them people alone."

"I don't know," Connie said. "Might be a little more complicated than that. My daddy used to tell me things about it. He used to read a lot on it. I read some on it too. I don't guess Custer really liked killing them Indians, women and babies and all."

"I don't know. Maybe he did, maybe he didn't." The old

man paused. He didn't turn away from the graveyard. "I don't reckon them bums much minded killing Kenny."

Connie smiled. "It ain't the same thing. I'm talking about fighting a war here. I'm talking about a general in the U.S. Army who was trying to fight in a war."

"And this man Custer, he didn't like killing them Indians?"

"Probably not. Sometimes a man figures he's got to do something even if he don't like it."

"That what your daddy said?"

"I don't know. I guess."

"Well, that's okay if it's the right thing to do." The old man put a leg up, climbed over the fence, and started walking out through the graves.

Connie climbed over after him and followed him onto a carriage path. On his left he passed a huge mausoleum that said DANNENBERG 1910 over the doors and just beyond it a marble angel or a woman. From the top of the hill the graveyard opened up into a huge series of desolate and gentle hills. It was all very beautiful — the layers of shadow the moon cast over the stones and terraces — but sobering too. Connie liked the stillness of it, the deep, quiet emptiness.

The path sloped downhill past terraces of smaller stones — obelisks, crosses, marble tablets and slabs surrounded by black wrought-iron fences. Connie tried to take it all in, to put his finger on the way the darkness made it beautiful, dimmed everything toward perfection, but the old man walked quickly and it was all he could do to keep up. Then halfway down the hill the old man stepped into the shadow of a giant oak and stopped behind an obelisk. The lettering was faint, but Connie could make out the word PIERCE.

From here he could see a large part of the cemetery. Up on the far hill to his right was the tile roof of the office and the top of the main gate into Rose Hill, and just in front of that stood a huge mausoleum, all gray in the moonlight. From there the cemetery tumbled in hills toward the river —

a dense scattering of monuments and mausoleums, occasional patches of oak and cedar black against the hills.

"How come you asked me about that man Custer?"

"No reason, I just thought of him. I remembered going with my daddy to the place where he died."

"Where's that?"

"Southeast Montana, not far from Wyoming. Little place called Hardin, on the Crow reservation. Hard On, that's what they called it."

"That's where you was from?"

"Naw, we lived way over on the other side of the state. My daddy took us down there one time on a trip. He souped up a car for somebody, or something like that. But I was born in Texas. My daddy, he used to run stock cars, but he smashed up and couldn't do that no more. I was about two or three, I guess. That's when we moved to Montana. His brother had a garage up there."

"I been to Montana," the old man said. "I'm just about sure of it. And I know I been to Texas. I remember lots about Texas. East Texas, awful hot and dusty." He looked off to his left, down a carriage path that ran along the top of the ridge. "That girl that makes them hamburgers, she something special to you?"

"That's right."

He nodded his head, still staring down the carriage path. "I believe I like her. I believe she's all right. You gonna get married?"

"Maybe."

"How come maybe? You don't want to?"

Sometimes Connie thought that was all he wanted. "Yeah, I want to."

"She don't want to then?"

A little fear went through him. He didn't want to think about that. "Well, you can't just get married. You gotta have something, you know. You gotta make a living."

"You don't make a living?"

"I will. I ain't worried about it."

"I fell for this woman once. She had that red hair too. I remember she was good at singing."

"Yeah?" Connie said. "What kinda singing?"

The old man looked at Connie, his face half hidden in the shadow of a low branch. "You know a song goes, *There's a land beyond the river*?"

"Nope."

"Good song. *There's a land beyond the river, that they call the sweet forever.* That kinda singing. She was good at it."

"I don't know that one."

"I don't remember much, but I remember them songs. Some of 'em all the way through. Most of 'em was about rivers. I remember that too. Singing about, that's what rivers are for. She said that, I think. There's another one goes, *I'll meet you in the morning by the bright riverside*. She liked singing about rivers. That's what rivers are for. She said that."

"And all this time," Connie said, "I just thought they was for fish to live in."

The old man slapped his thigh. "You don't know too much, do you."

"I never said I did."

"I know it. That's one of your good points. And you give me a shirt and bought me something to eat, so that's two more."

"And rivers ain't for fish to live in?"

"I never said that neither. I see 'em down here every day catching fish. Not right down by the graveyard, but down there under the bridge. I'm gonna get me some fish hooks and some line. Fish is good to eat."

Connie looked down into the graveyard rolling off toward the river and thought of his father standing knee-deep in a trout stream, his line whipping back behind his head and out into the water. "Trout," he said. "Trout's what's good. I was just about raised on trout."

The old man laced his fingers together and cracked his knuckles. "Catfish. Ain't no trout in that river."

"I was talking about Montana."

"Catfish is good too, though. But then you gotta get you a knife to clean 'em with. And a frying pan to cook 'em in. One thing always leads to another, don't it? You can't get away with having just a little something, one thing always leads to something else. Either have it all, or don't have nothing."

Connie looked up toward the main gate, the huge brick arch over the entrance to the cemetery. He couldn't see it clearly, but it seemed to be open. He thought then about Carl. This might be just the place Carl was looking for. It was deserted enough, and from a couple of these hills you could see just about the whole graveyard. Then he remembered hitting the boy, the jolt of anger, his fist balling, then the jolt again and the sharp rap to the face, the blood running from the boy's nose. That was an awful thing to do, and he was sorry for it. But he had to show him he meant business. He had to show him he could do what needed to be done. He wasn't going to let Carl down again. One thing the old man said was true. If you can't trust anybody, what's the use? And Carl was trusting him not to fuck this up. Everything else aside, Carl was still his brother and Carl was trusting him, and he wasn't going to let Carl down. "What's beyond that far hill over there?"

"More hills, more graves."

"How many?"

"'Bout as many as you're looking at now. Maybe more."

Connie let the thought settle in his head. This might be just the sort of place Carl needed. Pick the right time and this could be perfect. "Listen, I got to get rolling, pal. I got places to be."

"Not yet," the old man said. "You follow me on down here a piece. I got something for you."

"Naw, I really got to go now. I got —"

"You come on. It ain't far. I'm gonna show you my place. I got some stuff and I got something for you." The old man walked ten or fifteen yards down the narrow carriage path, then stopped and looked back over his shoulder. "You come on. It won't take long."

Connie started after him. "Then I got to go, all right?"

"You come on."

The trees hanging over the path made a wide awning and they walked under it, the old man a few yards ahead of Connie. They were walking lower into the valley now, along the side of a ridge. A hundred yards down the path the bricked walls of the terraces rose higher than Connie's head, and to his right the valley deepened. All around them tall marble gravestones stood up out of the hill, but Connie could read only a few names — LAMAR, BACON, ELLIS, and at the foot of a marble woman in a long flowing robe, the name BOZEMAN.

Then the valley dropped off steeply into a stand of thick hardwoods and brush. On his left Connie noticed the concrete wall of a terrace scratched with graffiti — a rough swastika buried under a peace symbol, the breasts and hips of a headless woman, a star with a circle around it, the word AMAZONS. Vandals. A beautiful place — the hills, the statues, the terraces — and somebody had to fuck it up. He hated that. Then, near the end of the wall, testimonies to another need, dozens of names and initials — CT LOVES BIG T, Liz/Jeri, STEVE DIES FOR GAIL.

Connie hurried his steps. They were walking now toward the point of the ridge, and halfway into the curve that would take them there, he could see on that point four or five huge marble monuments tucked among the oaks and magnolias. Forty yards short of those trees, the old man turned to his right and started to climb down a steep hill.

The half moon floating low over the tops of the far pines threw a bridge of dull gold on the river. It shimmered in the current but hung in place, as though it were anchored on both banks. The railroad tracks ran along the near bank, and just where they entered the trees at the far edge of the cemetery, a small fire burned.

"That's them," the old man said, climbing down the hill, holding on to scrub brush and the low limbs of oaks. "Tramps, hobos. That's yard speed down there. They come in on them freights."

Connie followed him down, half stumbling and half sliding, holding on to whatever he could find. "What they want a fire tonight for? I'm sweating like a pig."

"Bums always got fires. Someplace to hang out."

At the bottom of the hill the land flattened into a wide triangular gorge — grassy banks on two sides and on the third the graveyard sloping down to the river. A narrow creek ran out of the far bank and down the middle of the gorge, and beyond the creek, huge brick and marble crypts were cut into the face of the bank.

"Up this way," the old man said.

Connie followed him up the gorge and into a thicket of brush and small trees. They seemed to be moving toward the point where the two sides of the gorge converged, but in the thicket the moon was no help. Connie could barely see the back of the old bum's shirt weaving through the brush. After thirty yards, the old man got down on his knees and waited for Connie to catch up. They crawled another ten yards through thick undergrowth.

The old man motioned with his hand. "You wait a minute here," he said. He pulled back a large magnolia branch heavy with gray blossoms and crawled under it.

Connie squatted on his heels. He could hear the creek rustling through the gorge and what he thought was the river whispering along the foot of the hill. From the woods across the river a bird made a funny call, then everything was quiet, only a slight wind rustling the brush. Connie sat still where the old man had told him. It was an eerie place, quiet and almost totally dark. Then a strange hiss and glow came into the branches, a circle of gold in the dark foliage, bright and flaring, and in the closer leaves of the magnolia branches he could see the delicate green network of veins.

The light dimmed some and steadied, and the hiss faded. "Come on in here," the old man said.

Connie pulled back the branches to find more branches. He pulled those down and faced a hole in the earth, the mouth of a cave burning orange. But it wasn't a cave. He knew that from the bars, stubs of iron bars jagging the mouth like rusty teeth.

"You come on in here, it's okay. Watch them bars, though, they'll scratch you bad."

Connie crawled under the branches. It was a round hole about four feet wide and it opened into a short passageway. He swung a leg between the stubs, lowered his head and climbed through.

"Come on in here, boy. This is a good place, ain't it?"

The passageway opened up into a fairly large room with a shallow pit in the center and a tall domed ceiling. Connie thought of a large igloo, only the walls were clay, and in the lantern light they looked almost pink. In the middle of the floor the old bum's sleeping bag lay on a mattress of folded newspaper, beside it the lantern, a black plastic flashlight, a few paper bags, and a metal box.

"I cleaned it up a lot," the old man said. "Used to be lots of broke bottles and stuff. But it's all right, now."

"You know what this is, don't you?" Connie said.

The old man gave him a quick glance, then looked down at his things scattered across the floor. "I ain't in nobody's way. I reckon it's been empty a good while."

Connie stood up and stretched his back. "Any spiders in here?"

"I ain't seen none."

"I don't much like spiders. Bugs is one thing, but I don't like spiders. I seen a lot of 'em too, spraying up under houses and all."

"Well, I ain't seen no spiders."

Connie examined the walls. "You ever wonder who was in here or what happened to 'em?"

"Ain't no telling. Somebody probably moved 'em off. But that was a long time ago. I bet don't three people in this whole town even know about this place now."

The hole was already closing in. Connie stretched again and took a deep breath. The air smelled like a basement or the inside of a well. "Could be," he said. "This place is hid good enough."

"That's right. Can't see it from nowhere, and nobody's got no reason to be prowling around back here."

"How'd you find this place anyhow?"

"Kenny showed me. This is his lantern here."

"The guy that got killed."

"That's right. I already told you about Kenny." The old man shook his head. "He was a good boy."

"How you know they tossed him in the river?"

"They might have. He had him some money. He said they was after it, them tramps down at the river."

"Maybe he just pulled out. Caught one of those freights."

"Not without his lantern and his flashlight, he didn't. He wouldn't go off without his stuff. Kenny, he was sort of a hippie, but he wouldn't run off without his stuff."

"Ain't no more hippies, pal."

"Well, you take Kenny, he was what's left of 'em, I guess. He had a mouth harp, and he wore one of them rags on his head. And then he had him this long yellow ponytail. Pretty nice boy, liked to tell stories about things. He was good at telling stories."

"What kinda stories?"

"Oh, this and that. Where he'd been and all. He'd been all

over. Me too, I guess. Only I can't remember much about it no more. Kenny, he was sharp, he could tell it all." The old man sat down on the sleeping bag and crossed his legs under him.

"How long you been sleeping in here?"

"I don't know. Not long. Cozy, ain't it?"

"Too cozy for me," Connie said. "Like being locked up in a closet."

"You got somewhere else to sleep, though. I ain't."

Connie didn't say anything, only tried to imagine sleeping in the dark surrounded by these walls, this ceiling and floor, tried to imagine what it would be like to be sealed up in this place, the stuffy air going to absolutely nothing. He didn't like the thought.

"Sit down," the old man said.

"I'm all right." Something moved on the wall behind the old man's head. It moved again and disappeared into his shadow. "You sure there ain't no spiders in here?"

"I ain't seen none."

"I don't like spiders. My brother, when I was five or six, he used to put spiders in my bed. Sometimes I'd wake up in the middle of the night with a spider crawling on my face."

"Ain't no spiders in here," the bum said. "Sit on down. It ain't so bad. Keeps the rain off. And when you go to sleep you don't worry about nobody knocking your skull in with a rock. Beats jail too. You can come and go when you take the notion."

Connie shook his head. "I don't like jail neither."

"Aw, jail's all right," the old man said. "I been in a lot worse places. You just can't leave when you want to, that's all. But sometimes I think one place is about as good as another."

Connie looked over at the old man. "I appreciate the tour, pal, but I really gotta go now."

"Hold on a minute here."

"No, I really —"

"Naw, wait a minute. I got something to give you." The old man reached across the dirt floor and picked up the metal box. It was a small red box, the kind fruitcakes come in, but a lot of the paint had chipped off and it was rusting. He pried off the top and dug around inside. "Here," he said, holding out his hand.

Connie opened his palm and felt the old bum drop something into it. He held it down toward the lantern. It was a coin, a dirty one. And maybe an old one too, but the date was worn smooth. He tilted it toward the lantern. On one side was the picture of a bearded man in an odd helmet, on the other an eagle sitting on top of a big shield. The eagle had seven stars over its head. Most of the writing was worn away, but what was left looked foreign. "What is this thing?"

"I don't know. I had 'em a long time. Ain't nothing special. I got three of 'em. I'm giving you this one."

"Where'd you get it?" Connie said, still turning the coin over in his hand, studying the details.

"Who knows. It was a long time ago. Maybe it was your place, Montana. I believe I had them pieces most all my life. Used to carry 'em in my pocket, then I got scared I'd lose 'em."

"I bet it wasn't Montana."

"Some other place then. It don't much matter. Texas, California, Hawaii, Mexico, South America."

"Yeah," Connie said. "Looks like something foreign. Probably ain't worth much, but you can't never tell. Can't see what it's made out of, but it don't weigh much. Ain't gold or silver, that's for sure."

"Yeah, I know that."

"It's old, though, so you might be able to sell it at a pawnshop or something."

"Nope, it ain't worth nothing."

"You know that for a fact?"

"It ain't worth nothing, but you take it anyway. Take it for a lucky piece, or a memory piece, or whatever."

Connie rubbed the coin in his hand. He nodded.

The old man leaned back against the clay wall, his face almost pink in the lantern light.

5

CONNIE PLUGGED the tub, turned the hot and cold taps to a medium cool, and walked into the kitchen for a beer. He took a can of Pabst from the six-pack on the cabinet, then put the others in the fridge. He felt better already, and it wasn't just the air conditioner. There was something about Rita's place that really appealed to him. It was one small room, a half kitchen, and a bathroom in an old apartment building in a downtown neighborhood, but the tall ceilings and bright walls gave it a feeling of openness. The wallpaper was a soft yellow, comfortable and warm but not stifling, and the trim was a sky blue, like a bright ribbon on a package. The place always looked like it had just been cleaned, but Rita kept her things neat in a comfortable way — throw rugs and pillows on the dull oak floor, the pink flamingo smoothed tight on the yellow chenille bedspread.

There was a nice hominess here, a hominess that wasn't suffocating. He couldn't quite explain it, but he liked it. Even in the one room, with the one window, he didn't feel cramped. He thought it had to do with being artistic, with being good at arranging things, which Rita was, but he couldn't carry it much beyond that. Except to say that there was an economy about the place, a spareness. But it was a special sort of spareness, as though everything in the room —

the brass bed and night table, the rocking chair, the portable TV, the stereo, the Allman Brothers poster on the wall — as though each of these things had been chosen with great deliberation and care. Here was the home of a woman who didn't have very much or room for much, but what she had counted. And everything in the place made him feel as though he counted too. Everything here was special, and it was special because the person who lived here cared about herself. Connie liked that. He cared about her too. And being in Rita's place made him want to deserve to be there.

All of this, he knew, was what he wanted. Only he wanted it on a much larger scale. What Rita had made for herself in this tiny apartment he wanted them both to make for themselves somewhere else — in a nice house on a piece of land, a place to spread out and grow, a place to have something green. A log house, maybe, two-story, with a wide front porch and a deck off the back, a yard with shade trees thinning out into fields, a family place, a place where there would always be room to build more. Carl was right about one thing. You didn't build the kind of place he wanted in a trailer park.

Connie popped the top on the Pabst and walked back into the bathroom. The tub wasn't quite half full, but he set the can of beer on top of the toilet and stripped. Not having a tub was one of the real poverties of trailer living. On a hot day he liked nothing better than a long cool soak in the tub. There was nothing very relaxing about a shower. A shower was for saving space, for convenience. Its sole purpose was to wash off the dirt. A tub was a pleasure, a place to relax, to pamper the body. And this one was a real beauty, a deep old-fashioned tub on legs. He could run enough water into this one to swim in.

He dipped a foot — a little cool, but very nice — then stepped all the way into the tub, turned back the knobs, and eased down into the water. The cold ran up his thighs and made the hair on his stomach stand up. He sat for a second, letting his body adjust, then sank down into the tub and let the water run over his chest. He folded his legs Indian style and lay back, watching the thick mat of black hair sway in the water. What was it the old man had said about rivers? He felt a little like singing now. The rivers he remembered best were the Clark Fork, the Bitterroot, and the Blackfoot, the quick water fishermen in Montana stepped into with flyrods in their hands. That was what real rivers were for — the fly drifting in the current, the rainbow and the cutthroat hovering over the rocks. In Macon there was only the Ocmulgee, and it was always a shitty brown. Hardly anyone ever fished it, white people anyway. And nobody he knew ever fished it for sport.

Connie reached up for his beer and took a swallow. He thought again about what the old man had said and wondered if the woman who sang the songs might have been his wife. Maybe, though it was hard to believe a man like that might actually have had a wife. Hard to believe he might have had anything other people have, any kind of life at all except the daily rummaging through garbage cans, the panhandling, the sleeping in alleys and fields. Connie took another sip of his Pabst. He held it on his tongue for a second, then swallowed. What in the world brought people to the place the old man was?

Money. No, not just that. Luck? He didn't guess the old man had much of that, three coins or not. But you couldn't really tell. Maybe the old guy should have been dead three lives ago, face down in some alley with a knife in his back. He thought about the sleeping bag lying open in the center of the grave, the lantern turning the walls and roof an eerie shade of pink — that was probably the strangest place he'd ever been. Yes, it was certainly the strangest place he'd ever been. And remembering it now, Connie liked the old man. If he hadn't been sure of it then, he was sure of it now. The old guy knew what he was and he was up front about it, honest. He was glad to get the shirt, glad to get the hamburgers. And he gave back some of what he had. Connie liked that. He hated to see anybody get down that far, but most folks would steal you blind or slit your throat. There was something different about the old man. Connie remembered the way he'd acted at the Waffle House, how he didn't want to cause a stir, how he wanted to do everything just right. Then he remembered the fat guy in the yellow shirt. A first-class bastard. Maybe he should've laid him out, sent him to the doctor. No, what would that have accomplished. But the jerk shouldn't have shot his mouth off like that. There was no reason to talk that way. The old man hadn't done anything. He wasn't hurting anybody. Maybe the bastard thought he was showing off for Rita, or maybe even for his pals. Or maybe he was just in a shit mood. What had the old man said about people? It's a real mix? Maybe so, maybe some people just naturally caused other people trouble.

The phone rang. He sat up in the tub, then stopped. Forget it, let it ring. Then he thought again. It might be Rita. So he stood up, toweled off his face, and dried his feet on the mat. He wrapped the towel around his hips and walked into the bedroom.

"Hello," he said.

"Rita there?" It was a man's voice.

"Who is this?"

"Somebody calling for Rita, is she there?" It was that Maddox guy, the painter. Connie recognized his voice, a high whine, flat and nasal, as though his sinuses were shot.

"Listen, she don't wanna talk to you. Why don't you just fuck off?"

"Why don't you just let me talk to Rita, okay? I've got something important to tell her."

"Fuck off."

"Listen, is she there? This is important."

Connie didn't say anything. He was getting angry.

"Okay, then, I guess she's at work. I'll just call down there."

The line clicked dead and Connie hung up the phone. He was trying not to get worked up. He looked across the room at the paintings leaning against the wall — a couple of beach scenes, the face of a man in dark glasses, the long legs of a woman in red high heels. She wasn't bad, he guessed. The colors in some of them were nice. But she wasn't all that good either, not so he could tell. He wondered if everything the guy had told her was just to get her into the sack, the business about the art lessons, the talk about school in Atlanta. Connie shook his head. He knew about wanting something — it always sounds like the corniest line in the world till somebody tells it to you.

And if it's what you wanted to hear, he knew the things you'd do to make it happen. He hadn't told Rita, but he'd seen the photos of her in the black lingerie, the garter belt and hose. And the one photo taken of her on her knees, at arm's length, only slightly blurred. That one just about made him crazy. What kind of lies did the guy have to tell her to get her to do that? He'd thought about confronting her with them. He'd thought about dragging them out of the drawer and sticking them all over the walls, but he could never justify having prowled through her dresser.

Besides, Charles Maddox was still a very sore point with Rita. One night Connie had seen them together at the Steak & Egg on Forsyth and had made a messy scene. They were sitting in a booth in the side room, on the same side of the table, Maddox wedging Rita close to the wall. Connie saw them as he walked in to check the racks for a pool cue. A look of alarm went across her face, then she caught herself and tried to cover it up, tried to look innocent. She waved him over to the table to introduce them. Connie walked over, but only to give them both a bad look. When Maddox held out his hand to shake, Connie slapped it away and went back into the poolroom.

For days after that Rita gave him the serious business. But

he gave it right back. Why did she want to screw around with a guy like that? Maddox was fifty if he was a day, and he looked like he did drugs. Some things, she said, he'd never understand, but he ought not to flaunt his ignorance. Connie hated that. He didn't like to be talked down to, to be made to feel inferior. He called Maddox a washed-up faggot of a painter, if he was even that. And he told her if he ever heard the guy had laid a finger on her, he'd break his face. But Connie knew it was an idle threat. He knew she'd already been doing things for him — twice, at least, she'd spent the night with him. Connie knew that for a fact. One night he'd called her very late and when she didn't answer her phone, he looked up the guy's address in the phone book, drove over to his house, and found her Plymouth in the driveway. A week later he found it there again. Charles Maddox. It turned his stomach to think about him. How did a girl like Rita get mixed up with a vulture like that?

He walked back into the bathroom, dropped the towel on the lid of the toilet, and climbed back into the tub. The cool water felt good again spreading up his legs and hips. It was almost enough to calm him down. He lay back and remembered wading once in a creek in Plains, Montana, sitting on the rocks as the mountain water rushed over him. He was young then, eight or nine, and not much of the memory was left — only the cool water moving over the smooth rocks, the cliff rising over one side of the creek, the deep blue sky, and downstream his father and Carl wading in hip boots. Then he remembered they were arguing about something, two grown men shouting and pushing each other in the middle of the creek. That was all of the memory, but the best parts of it were still good — the water, the rocky cliff, the sky.

Connie thought Rita might like Montana. It was wide open and clean, beautiful in the spring and summer, the mountains turning bright green under the snowcaps, the sky a pure blue, the rivers swelling with the snowmelt and running clear as glass all summer. The winters were hard, but they could deal with that. He remembered being stuck once on the highway in a ground blizzard — dead still in the middle of the highway, his mother starting to panic, and all around them nothing but snow, almost as if someone had painted all the windows white. They'd have to learn to deal with such stuff, but they could do that. Other people did it, so they could do it too.

What he wanted was a place in the mountains, a piece of land, nobody else around for miles. That could be a fine way to live — alone, doing for themselves, building something up out of a little piece of ground. It appealed to Connie, the notion of working together, of two people building the sort of place Rita had built here, only much bigger, a log house on a good piece of ground, a few horses, some cattle, maybe even some burros or sheep. They could learn about things like that. And if Carl could pull this off, they'd have a good start. And Carl could pull it off too. Connie was sure of it. If Carl didn't hurt the kid, everything would work out just fine. And he wouldn't do that. Carl was a lot of bark, but he'd never really hurt him. He couldn't, it wasn't in him. They'd just take the money and split, phone the kid's mother from two or three hundred miles away and tell her where to find him. He knew it was that simple, and he knew Carl would make it work, but he still had a bad feeling about it. It was the kid, he thought. It was because he'd hit him when his hands were cuffed. And the kid would hardly go a hundred and twenty. That wasn't like him. It was too much like hitting a woman.

Carl was right about one thing, though. Where else could two people like Connie and Rita get enough money to make a good start? He thought about that for a second. Yes, Carl was right. He didn't want to see anybody get hurt and he was sorry for the kid. He truly was. He knew the last few days had been terrible for him. But if everything went right, the kid'd be okay, Carl would be okay, and he and Rita would be better than that. Sure, the kid's old lady would be out a few bucks, but it wasn't like she couldn't afford it. Carl said she owned half of Jacksonville.

He picked up the soap and washed his face, underarms, and crotch. It was a yellow heart-shaped bar, and it smelled a little too much like flowers. No, Carl wouldn't hurt him. And it wasn't a bad plan entirely, not if you thought about it, though it wasn't the sort of thing he'd get himself into on purpose. But Carl had done it, and he guessed it wouldn't do to worry about that now. The thing to do now was make it go smooth and get what he could out of it. And Carl was right, it was a good chance for him and Rita to make a start. Montana might be just the place. A little piece of land up around Plains, or maybe a little farther down the road toward Paradise. Connie smiled. He remembered his mother, the steel trestle bridge over the Clark Fork, a joke she used to make. Every time they'd cross it going home she'd say, "Just over this river I'll bet we'll find Paradise." And it was always there, the same four run-down buildings — the Burlington Northern depot, the grocery store, the café, the Pair-A-Dice Bar. He remembered the way she laughed when they hit the end of the bridge and the town opened up in front of them. He knew now that it was a laugh at the whole family, a laugh at bad times. But even when the joke was worn out, when they all knew that Paradise never changed, it was still good-humored, a laugh filled with love for everyone in the car. Plains or Paradise, or somewhere in between, it hardly mattered. There were so many mountains and valleys, so much space, and so few folks to fill it. With a little money to spend, anybody could get lost up there.

He slid down in the tub, held his nose, and dunked his head all the way under the water. His ears clogged and the world went pleasantly away. Rita might really like Montana — the mountains and the rivers, the antelope, elk, deer, bear, buffalo. If you couldn't paint pictures in a place like Montana, you couldn't paint pictures anywhere. He'd remember to tell her that. And they could live for a good while before either one of them had to get a job. Yes, he'd remember to tell her that too. He came up out of the water, shook out his ears, and wiped his eyes. It was all a matter of looking at it the right way. If you looked at it the right way, the whole business made a lot of sense.

Connie picked up his beer, took a long swallow, and sank back down into the tub. He had a troubling thought about Carl. He supposed he wouldn't see him for a while. Maybe Carl would go up to New York. He knew a woman up there. Sure, Carl was made for New York — the sharp clothes, the nightclubs. "The Big Apple," he was always calling it. Then again, where Carl would get to was anybody's guess. He needed to talk to him about that. Carl was rough sometimes, but he was all right. No, he was rough all the time, he'd always been rough. But Carl was his only brother and had taken care of him, had raised him since he was twelve or so, and Carl barely old enough to get a job and keep it. He owed Carl a lot, he knew that. And he wanted to do this thing right. He worried about him, about what Tommy might do if Carl couldn't pay him the money. But all of this would be behind them in a few days. Then the whole business would be just another bad spot in a road that led to a good place. Another bump on the road to Paradise. He tried to smile but without much luck. It was the kid. It was because he'd hit the kid in the face. He kept seeing the bruised lip against the pale skin. Odd how that worked. He'd hit a hundred guys in the face, had seen his own face so bruised and swollen he hardly knew himself in the mirror. But hitting the kid was different. It was a shameful feeling, like somebody catching you jerking off. He took another long swallow of the beer and set the empty can on top of the toilet. In Montana they'd have a big tub, maybe even a whirlpool.

The shampoo smelled like flowers too, but he used it anyway. After he rinsed his hair, he pulled the plug, stood up, and dried himself off. He wished he'd gone by his trailer for some clean clothes. But it probably wasn't a good idea. Carl might be right about Tommy having the place watched. It wasn't likely, but it was possible. He thought about the cop asking questions about Carl. Maybe he shouldn't have gone to the Waffle House, but what the hell. He thought about going downstairs and washing his clothes, but he couldn't even do that. He didn't have anything else to put on. There was Carl's new underwear in the car, but he wasn't going back out for it. Then he remembered the blue shirt. He'd have to go back out to the lodge without the shirt. Carl wouldn't be very happy. He'd have to make up some kind of story, a really good story, tell him he'd go out in the morning and buy another one. Connie dreaded the thought. He walked naked into the kitchen and got another Pabst from the fridge.

Walking through the cool apartment felt good, and he stood for a moment in the center of the room, letting the air conditioner dry the last damp spots on his body. He switched on the TV. It buzzed and flickered, then turned into a black and white island swarming with Japanese soldiers. Artillery blasts chunked up the beach and the palms edging the jungle. A plane swooped down and strafed the tree line, and a huge gun went off on the deck of a ship. Connie propped the pillows at the head of the bed and turned off the overhead light. He set the can of beer on the night table and lay down.

"Hello, baby," the voice said, quiet, almost a whisper. The bed sank with the weight of another body, and a hand brushed through his hair. "Hello, baby," the voice said again.

He opened his eyes to the dark room and saw her in the light of the TV. Her body was naked and gray in the silver light. She leaned over him and kissed him on the chin, then she kissed his chest and moved her tongue down his stomach.

He felt a stir in his crotch. Then the touch of her lips, and he felt himself growing.

He took a deep breath and rubbed his eyes, turned his head on the pillow and looked at the clock on the night table. The soft green numbers said 12:12, then flipped to 12:13. "I gotta go," he said.

But she didn't stop.

"I gotta go. I told Carl I'd meet him somewhere."

She stopped then, but held him firmly in her hands. "Not just yet," she said, her voice still a whisper. And she slid up on top of him and eased him inside her.

When Connie woke again, light had seeped in through the lace curtains and brightened half the room. Rita lay asleep beside him, the sheet kicked down around her legs, the diamondback shadow of the lace draped like a shawl across her shoulders.

He sat up and leaned over toward the window, pulled aside the curtain. Down below the rickety balcony and balustrade, the trees in the little park that divided Orange Street flared bright green. The black wrought-iron benches already looked hot, and so did the bricks in the street. Across the park the sun lit the front of the old Allman Brothers house — the first place the band had lived when they moved to Macon, a bright yellow two-story house with white columns on the porch. Rita's sister had gone out with one of the roadies, and Rita liked to talk about that. She liked to put on an album and tell Connie the stories she'd heard about traveling around the country with the band. They were good stories, a part of her sister's recklessness she actually admired. The poster on her wall was a blown-up photo taken backstage at the Fillmore East. Elizabeth had a whole book of them, photos taken at every concert they did the year after their first album. Next to Otis Redding, she said, the Allmans were the biggest thing that ever happened in Macon. When Duane crashed his bike, it was like the end of an era.

Rita shifted and rolled onto her side, away from the window. She was not a beautiful woman, but she was attractive. Her nose was a little large, but not terribly. And Connie liked the dimple in her chin. Mostly, though, he liked her deep green eyes and thick lashes, the way her high cheekbones made them look a little dramatic. She talked a lot with her eyes, the way some people talk with their hands, and he liked to watch her when she got excited about something.

Her eyes moved now under their smooth lids. Connie reached up and brushed her hair away from her cheek — red hair, fine and straight. Five tiny gold rings shone up the edge of her right ear. He liked those rings, and he didn't like them. He liked them because they looked exotic climbing from her lobe halfway up her ear, something out of a magazine or a movie. He didn't like them because they hadn't been there before she met Maddox.

She opened an eye and closed it again.

Connie watched her eyes, the little movement under the lids. Her mouth was slightly open on the pillow and her breathing was slow and even. He reached up gently and touched the earring hanging in her lobe. It was hardly more than a gold wire — delicate and simple — but Connie thought it was very beautiful. It reminded him of a delicate bird, a canary or a parakeet.

It occurred to him then that what he felt for her was something he may have never actually felt for another woman. Their times together were always good, but it wasn't the good feeling that made him understand this. There had been good feelings with other women, several of them, though they'd never lasted very long. No, it wasn't the good feeling that made him understand this. It was the bad, the awful pain that hit him whenever he thought about losing her. He knew this was true. It was the pain he felt, not the joy, that put the real value on his life with her. And it was a pain that was almost unbearable, worse than any beating he'd ever taken in the ring. In a fight he could take almost anything from anybody.

He could toughen up and stand it. But this pain was so much worse. Every time he saw the five gold rings, every time he thought of her car parked in the painter's driveway, he caught a glancing blow from it. And it was more than enough to show him that if this pain ever hit him full force, if it ever caught him solid, there'd be no getting up.

He turned the earring over to see that it really did pass all the way through her ear.

"What are you doing?" she whispered.

"Nothing."

She rolled over onto her back, kicked the sheet off her legs, and put her hands under her pillow.

Connie smiled at the light fluffs of hair under her arms. Then he looked at her breasts, the narrow pale stripes running across them. Those stripes of untanned skin made being with her more intimate. And he loved her breasts. They were small and beautiful, her nipples soft pink. He leaned down and kissed the left one.

"Now what are you doing?"

"You don't know?"

"What time is it?" She opened her eyes, closed them for a second, and opened them again.

"Little after nine."

She reached up, took his arm, and tried to pull him down to her. "Let's sleep a while longer."

"I got to go. I'm already in enough trouble."

"Trouble with who?"

He tried to push away from her. "Carl. He's gonna skin me alive."

She let go of him then and rubbed her eyes. She cleared the rasp from her throat and looked up at him. "Connie, what's all this Carl business about? Two guys came in last night asking about him."

"Them cops?"

"Two more guys. 'You seen Connie Holtzclaw?' they said.

'You seen his brother, Carl? Connie know where his brother is?'"

"What'd you tell 'em?"

"I told 'em the truth. 'Yeah, I've seen Connie. No, I ain't seen Carl. What do I care about Carl?'"

"What'd you tell 'em about me and Carl?" he said. "You tell 'em I know where Carl's at?"

"I didn't tell 'em nothing. I said, 'How do I know? He never talks about Carl.'" She propped up on an elbow. "So what's all this Carl business? I think you ought to tell me."

"Nothing much. Carl just lost some money, that's all."

"To Tommy Wilson?"

"Yeah, and some of Tommy's friends."

"How much?"

"I don't know. Maybe eight, maybe nine thousand."

"Jesus," she said. "You didn't lose any money, did you?"

"No, you crazy? I don't bet. You know that." The way she studied his face made him edgy.

"Okay," she said, "then what's this thing you been talking about with you and Carl? You tell me the truth."

He shook his head and looked out the window into the park. "That ain't got nothing to do with this. I ain't mixed up in that gambling shit. What I'm doing with Carl is a whole different thing." The sun was already a glaze on the brick street. He dreaded going out.

"So what is it exactly?"

"I can't tell you. We already been through that. It's sort of an investment. A secret investment."

"An investment?"

"Sort of." He swung his legs over the side of the bed, bent down, and picked up his shorts. They were rank and stiff with sweat, and he tossed them back to the floor.

"You're lying to me."

Connie turned and gave her a quick look. "No, I ain't. And I told you all I'm gonna tell you."

"Shitass," she said. "You tell me all these big shit plans, and I don't even know what the hell's going on. What am I supposed to think?"

"You ain't supposed to think nothing. Me and Carl's coming into a little money, that's all. Enough to set us up for a while. We can get the shit away from here. Montana maybe." He kicked his dirty shirt across the floor. "It's got to do with insurance, and that's all I'm saying. I ain't jinxing my luck. Every time I say too much I jinx my luck."

"Connie, you ain't jinxing nothing. You never had any luck to jinx." She dropped back onto the bed, folded her pillow, and propped it under her head.

"Well, I'm gonna have, goddamnit. And this is the time."

She lay quiet for a few seconds, her eyes narrowed, thinking. "And this is totally legitimate business, and it doesn't have anything to do with Tommy Wilson?"

"Totally legitimate."

"And it doesn't have anything to do with Tommy Wilson?"

"Not one goddamn thing. Unless he just happens to own the goddamn insurance company."

Rita studied his face again. "You swear it?"

"I swear it."

For a moment she seemed satisfied, then she sat up. "Then how come he's looking for you?"

"I told you, goddamnit, he ain't looking for me. He's looking for Carl." He stood up and picked up his jeans. "I don't have any clean underwear over here, do I?"

"You know, it's always Carl with you. Carl this, Carl that. I'm just about sick of Carl."

"He's my brother."

"And I'm sure he's got your best interest at heart."

Connie ignored her. "I got any clean underwear over here?"

She didn't say anything. She grew suddenly abstracted.

"Well," he said, "do I?"

"You know, if Carl told you to jump off a cliff, I think you'd ask him headfirst or what."

He felt himself tense. He lifted a hand. "Don't tell me about my brother, okay? You don't know a goddamn thing about my family."

"You call him family?"

"Listen," he said. "Don't you talk to me about family. I ain't locked nobody up in a nuthouse."

Rita's eyes hardened and her fist balled around the sheet. "Goddamn you, shitass. Nobody's locked anybody up in a fucking nuthouse. It's a fucking nursing home. It's a goddamn fucking nursing home."

He raised his eyebrows. "Sure it is."

"Goddamn you, asshole. You think I can afford to take care of her on what I make? You think Elizabeth sends me anything?" She clenched her jaws and stared at him. "Goddamn you *and* your goddamn fucking brother. You're both shitasses."

He hated it when she got this way. Watching her eyes redden made him feel mean and helpless, and sometimes it could take hours to calm her down. "Okay," he said. "Just don't talk to me about Carl, that's all."

"Goddamn," she said. "You just don't seem to get it. He's an asshole, Connie. And you just walk around as blind as a goddamn bat."

"Maybe that ain't for you to say, all right?" He tossed the jeans over the arm of the rocker and ran his fingers through his hair. "I got any clean underwear over here?"

Her eyes were still narrow and hard. "You don't even believe he made that pass at me, do you?"

"He was drunk, that's all. People get drunk."

"And that's some kind of excuse?"

Connie shook his head. "It was six fucking months ago. There was a lot of people there. He didn't even know you was with me."

"Hell, Connie, he saw us walk right through the goddamn door. And half an hour later, he sticks his hand up my dress?"

"He was drunk, goddamnit. Besides, he apologized, didn't he?"

"Fuck you. He apologized to you. He never apologized to me."

"Well, I apologized to you, didn't I?" He didn't need this. Not today, not on top of everything else. "I asked you if I got any underwear over here. So how 'bout it, do I?"

"I don't keep up with your underwear."

He pulled on his jeans, sucked in his stomach, and zipped. "Okay, I guess I just won't wear any."

Rita sat for a minute on the bed without saying anything, then she wiped her eyes on the sheet. When she looked back up at him, her face had softened some. "So go by the damn trailer and change. You got enough time to do that, don't you?"

"Carl said not to. Tommy's watching his place. He figures he might be watching the trailer too."

"Great," she said. "So that's why you're over here."

"Naw. I ain't been over there for a couple of days. We got a place."

"Great," she said again. "And that's all I get outta you?"

"I already told you about this, didn't I?"

She looked at the shorts and shirt on the floor. "You want me to wash those for you?"

"Naw, the hell with it. I ain't got time. I should've washed them last night, I guess."

She rubbed her eyes on the sheet again, then pointed toward her dresser. "Look over there in that top drawer. I think I got one of your T-shirts in there. It's one of those red ones."

Connie stepped over and opened the drawer. Folded on top of her nightgowns lay one of his old workout shirts. In faded white letters it said, JACKIE'S GYM. He didn't really want to wear it, but his other shirt was too rotten to put back on.

"How come you didn't tell me Charles called last night?"

"I don't know." He slipped the shirt over his head. "I forgot, I guess. I was asleep when you came in."

"He called the Waffle House. Said you wouldn't tell him whether I was home or not."

"Fuck him. He lied. I told him you were at work."

She gave him a long look. "And why would he lie about something like that?"

"He knows I don't like him, and he don't like me neither. That's reason enough." Connie tucked the T-shirt into his jeans. "You got any corn flakes or anything?"

"You tell me when people call. You hear that? I like to get all my messages."

"I forgot, okay? Anyhow, he called you, didn't he?"

Rita didn't follow it up, only played for a second with an earring. "I'm out of cereal. You want me to fry you some eggs?"

"I ain't got time."

"It won't take a minute."

"No." He plopped on the edge of the bed, leaned down, and slipped his bare feet into his tennis shoes.

She slid over close and put her hands on his back. "So when you coming around again?"

"I don't know. Soon. A couple of days, maybe."

When she started rubbing his shoulders, he sat up. She rubbed hard, kneading the muscles between her thumbs and fingers. "I thought maybe we could do something tomorrow. It's Easter."

"Easter?" he said.

"Yeah, Easter. You know, bunnies, Easter baskets, colored eggs? Church? Easter, you get it?"

"So?"

"So people do things on Easter."

"Like what?"

"Like go places. I thought we might go somewhere. We never go anyplace. You ever notice that?"

"Sure we do. We go all sorts of places."

She stopped rubbing. "No, we don't. I bet we haven't been to a movie in a goddamn month."

"So where you wanna go?"

She let her hands drop and fell back onto the bed. "Anyplace, Connie. The park. Anyplace."

"What park?"

"Any goddamn park. I just meant someplace. Any damn place."

"I'd like to," he said, "but I don't know where I'll be tomorrow. I might be around, and I might not. It's hard to say."

Her voice took on a slight edge. "So when do you think you'll be around for sure?"

"I don't know. A couple of days or so, I guess. It's hard to tell, but this business'll be over soon. Then we can really go somewhere. We can get outta this shithole." He turned and put his hand on her knee, and she jerked the leg away. "What the hell?"

"You're really something, you know that?"

"Listen, Rita, I'm doing this for both of us. It ain't no fucking vacation for me neither."

"You're something, that's all. I mean, what makes you think I'm going to give up what I got here and run off with you to God knows where for a reason you ain't even halfway figured out yet?"

"And what all you got here, huh? A damn job at the Waffle House."

"Yeah, well at least I can hold a job." She paused to let it sink in. "Besides, I might just quit that job and do something else."

"Like what? Go off to that school?"

She rolled onto her side and pushed up on an elbow. "Okay," she said. "Let's just not do this. I swear, it's wearing me out. It's like all we ever do is argue. And I just don't want to argue anymore. Not this morning, anyway."

"Hell, I ain't arguing. I'm just telling you about getting

outta here. About getting outta this town and getting someplace good for a change, someplace where we can have something like everybody else." He put his hand on her leg again,
and this time she didn't move. "Listen," he said. "I don't see
why you don't want us to have something. You wanna live in
this shithole town all your life?"

"It's not a shithole, Connie. It's a really nice place. No, it's
a beautiful place. Just drive around today and look at the
houses, okay? And the azaleas and the dogwoods. Just drive
down College Street and look at those old houses. They're
gorgeous, and a lot of 'em over a hundred years old. That
doesn't mean anything to you?"

"They can't mean nothing to me unless I live in one."

"I just think we've got a lot to talk about, that's all."

"Well, I don't. Montana's a great place. You can paint all
kinds of pictures in Montana. You ever think about that?"

"Connie, you just don't pick up and move someplace you
never been. You never think two goddamn steps ahead. You
gotta have a reason for going somewhere and something to
do when you get there."

"I been there before."

"For chrissake, Connie. Not since you were a kid."

"And I got a reason, too. I'm sick of this goddamn place."

"That ain't a reason. Or if it is, it's a reason for leaving
someplace. It ain't a reason for going someplace."

He thought about Charles Maddox. "Well, it's all the reason
I need. We'll get some horses to raise and maybe some sheep,
and you can paint all day if you want to."

"And towns change, Connie. It's probably not even the
same place."

"Places like Plains, Montana, don't change. Rivers don't
change and mountains don't change, and fish and birds and
deer don't change. And horses don't change either. Shit."

"And what am I supposed to tell my mama, huh? 'Oh, by
the way, I'm packing up everything and moving to Montana

with Connie Holtzclaw.' 'How nice, dear. And what does he do?' 'Oh, Mom, he's a successful businessman. He deals in secret investments.'"

"Tell her whatever you want to. Or don't tell her nothing. Hell, you ain't even talked to her in a year."

She kicked his hand away. "I talk to her every goddamn week. I talk to her every goddamn week on the goddamn telephone."

"Sure you do."

"I talk to her every goddamn week. You hear that?" She slid up on the bed and kicked at him with her heel. "You think I can just pick up every time I feel like it and drive down there? Some of us have to work, you know."

"Sure," he said. "Let's drop it. I just want us to have something good, that's all. I just want us to have what other people have. And with the money me and Carl got coming, we can have it out there."

She lay back on the bed and stared again at the ceiling.

Connie watched her stretch in the sunlight and thought again of the boy on the mattress. What in the world would she think of that? He watched her eyes trace the blue trim under the ceiling. After a while they began to soften. "You don't think we deserve that?" he said. "A good start?"

"My mama used to take me to Sunday school every Easter. I ever tell you about that?"

"No."

"You ever go to Sunday school?"

"Not much."

"I went every Sunday. I liked it. My mama took us, me and Elizabeth. We only lived three or four blocks from the church. On Easter they'd give you this little green plant. To take care of, you know. I used to keep one in the window in my room. It was in this little yellow pot, and the leaves always leaned toward the window. You could turn it all the way around and the next day it was leaning right back."

"Fuck, I'm talking about giving us a good start here, about having something." He grabbed her ankle and gave it a shake. "A goddamn house and some goddamn land to go with it."

She kicked him away again. "I'm talking about Easter, goddamnit. They'd give you these little green plants. And sometimes a flower. I ever get any flowers from you? On a goddamn birthday, or Valentine's Day, or Easter? It was nice, okay? It was goddamn nice."

"I'd rather have Easter eggs. You can eat them."

"It was something alive, stupid. New life, you get it? It was supposed to mean something."

He pushed off the bed. "Listen, when this is all over you'll have all the goddamn flowers you want. I'll see to it, all right? And I'll tell you about something meaning something. Anybody asks you again if I know where Carl is, you tell 'em no. You tell 'em I been looking for him myself. And you tell 'em like you mean it. You got that?"

"Sure," she said. "I got it."

6

WHEN THE OLD MAN opened his eyes to the dark of the grave, the last note of his dream retreated into a faint screeching of tin reeds. In the dream, Kenny hunched beside him over a fire, the mouth harp cupped to his lips, the brassy notes vibrating full and mellow through his fingers. He played "On Top of Old Smoky" and "Red River Valley," and there was a coffeepot on the fire and canned beans and Vienna sausage warming beside it. Over his shoulder the river ran between the graveyard and the pines, and above the pines the moon blushed orange as a pumpkin. After that, in the half dream of slow waking, Kenny's ghost haunted the graveyard with a funeral dirge. He harped the plaintive "Call Me Not Back" and danced a few steps on a granite slab, his face as bloodless as the stone he waltzed on. But now the old man tossing on the sleeping bag, awake and in possession of memory, knew the music sifting through the thicket, if you could call it music, was only the lame and boozed O'Brien. Maybe it was Kenny's harp he held to his lips, but it was only Crank O'Brien wandering along the carriage paths, his drunken breath stumbling over the reeds.

The old man stretched, folded his arms across his chest, and closed his eyes again. He listened to the thin screech of the harp from the graveyard and tried to drift back into his dream. It was useless. He only tossed. The pain in his joints had eased some overnight except for the dull throb in his hands and feet. He thought about the ten-dollar bill and considered buying a bottle of aspirin. A whole bottle would cost too much, three or four dollars. But for a dollar and a half you could get one of those little plastic boxes of Bayer. That was a dozen tablets. Also he wanted some batteries for the tape player. He hadn't changed the batteries in a long time, and he was afraid they might go dead soon. Already, he thought the tapes might be slowing down. The money, though, should be spent on food, on necessities. He knew that. Batteries were just too easy to slip into your pocket. All of the money should be spent on food. He'd find George and they'd go down to the Krystal. Then maybe to the Kroger to load up on soup and beans. He liked the Campbell's vegetable beef, the old-fashioned kind with the chunks of meat, and they'd get some chicken noodle for George too. Maybe even some soda crackers and a can of sardines. But he wanted to keep a dollar or so back. It was always good to know you had something to get at when you really needed it.

The mouth harp now was a chronic whine, and he pictured O'Brien perched on a gravestone, the heel of his cork leg propped on a terrace wall. Sometimes, says O'Brien, he can still feel the pain aching down the bone. Only there ain't no bone there no more, only hard cork whittled into a leg and a foot. On your granny's grave, says O'Brien, nothing won't help a pain like that — not drink, not dope, not medicine. 'Cause there ain't no leg for it to run to. The old man imagined O'Brien down on his back and straddling the rail. He didn't want to ride the cars anymore. He felt too old now, too stiff in the joints. Look at O'Brien lying there in the gravel with his stump kicking blood all over the track. You slip up jumping a freight and you wind up with a pain where there's nothing left to have a pain in. And what do you do about that? It was a strange circumstance, and it made you feel sorry for O'Brien, even if you knew what a snake he was, even if you knew he'd stab you in the ribs for a half-pint of hooch.

He felt in his pocket for the ten-dollar bill. It was empty, so was the left. Confused, he dug into the pocket of his shirt. There it was, a crisp fold of paper. He rubbed the bill between his fingers, took it out and unfolded it in the dark. It made a nice crinkling sound. A new bill, he guessed. That was a good kid, a shirt and a ten-dollar bill all in one night, and the hamburgers too. You couldn't expect treatment like that very often. He wadded the bill into a loose ball and stuffed it into the right-hand pocket of his jeans. It was less likely to fall out that way, and you could reach down, pat your pocket, and feel the edges of the money dig a little into your leg. If you ever had any paper money, that was a good way to carry it.

He wasn't hungry, but his stomach growled and he knew he'd need to eat before long. When the music stopped, he'd go out and try to find George. They'd walk down to the Krystal for hamburgers and fries, then over to the Kroger. But he had to wait till the music stopped. O'Brien must be somewhere close, and it wouldn't do for a snake like that to see him crawling out of the thicket. O'Brien wasn't one to show your place to.

Lying quietly in the pitch dark, the old man listened to the whine of the mouth harp, no distinguishable song, and thought of Kenny playing in his dream. He was glad to have the lantern and flashlight — they made the nights a lot easier — but he missed the good stories and the music. And Kenny was a boy with such a sweet face, a heart so warm it glowed in his eyes. And the way he could play that mouth harp — "Camptown Races," "Harvest Moon," "Down in the Valley" — such warmth in the notes, never anything fancy, just the straight and honest feeling. A lantern and a flashlight were no fair trade for that. But it wasn't good to trouble over it. Sufficient unto the day is the evil thereof. He thought of the tape player and the batteries. What he needed was some new music, something to take him to another time and place. Later on, he'd walk over to that shopping center, hit the Bible store and go through the tapes, maybe find one with a woman's voice.

The harp playing stopped. The old man sat up on the sleeping bag and listened. A wind played in the brush and the tops of the trees, but the mouth harp had stopped. He had to piss now, but he thought he should wait before he crawled out of the thicket. Wait awhile and listen, that was the best plan. Then piss and go for the hamburgers. George might be down at the camp, but you couldn't count on it. If he wasn't, he'd probably be downtown on the bum, maybe at the poolhall. Look around, but don't count on George. He might be halfway to Atlanta for all you know, pulled up and gone, and never a word to anybody.

"The singing nigger?" The bartender leaned around the corner of the bar and spit a wad of gum into a half-gallon peach can. "Yeah, he come in here 'bout an hour ago, drunk, talking that singing bullshit again. And I'll tell you something too. Joel T. Sullivan or nobody else ain't gonna give him no guitar, not unless he forks over some cash. And he's gotta nerve putting the touch on me."

All the shades were pulled and the only light was a string of beer signs on the wall behind the bar — two yellow mugs of Miller High Life, a red Budweiser wagon with a clock in the side. The old man could hardly see a thing. "Where'd he go to, he say?"

"You tell him Pink Raine ain't no Scrooge, all right? But he ain't no fool neither. Come in here singing that coon trash and wanting me to buy him a guitar. Street singing, shit. I got a reputation in this town and it ain't for being no fool."

"Say where he was going?"

The bartender pulled up the tail of his apron and wiped his mouth. "Hey, I heard you was dead. Where you been?"

"I ain't dead, I guess."

"Well, you might be yet. Varne says he's after you. How come you saying them things about him?" He dug a stick of Juicy Fruit out of his shirt pocket.

"I ain't done nothing to him, and I don't reckon he much minds telling a lie." The old man turned toward the door. He wasn't worried about any Varne. Big man Varne, he ain't bullying nobody. "George say where he was headed?"

The bartender pointed with the stick of gum. "I'll tell you who was with him too. That Willie Lipscomb. I don't admire neither one, drunk or sober. Too mean to be white men."

"So how 'bout George? He say where he was going?"

"Who knows? Try that nigger bar on Poplar Street."

The roses on the hill were beautiful and so were the dogwoods blooming above them, but the old man bypassed the main entrance and walked down to the gate that said OAK RIDGE. The day had warmed up to a broil and the aspirin he'd bought at the Rexall had eased the hurt in his hands and feet. He felt swell now with the sun on his shoulders, the hot concrete under his feet — sassy and nimble, a man with some blood in his veins. All he needed was chow and that wasn't far away. He'd check out the tracks one more time, and if George wasn't there, he'd hit the Krystal for burgers and fries.

If he couldn't figure where George had wandered off to, he wasn't going to fret. He'd walked down to Mulberry and looked in the poolhall, then down to a flophouse and two other bars on Broadway. Nobody else had seen him in days. Either George would turn up or he wouldn't, with the guitar or not. Still, the old man hoped someone would front him the money. George could get one at the pawnshop for twenty or thirty bucks. Maybe it wouldn't be the best guitar in the

world, but that didn't matter. George was good, a real blues-
man, and he could sing the gospel too. Sometimes when
Kenny played the harp, George would sing along. He had a
real voice, George did. A big mellow bass that rattled when
the songs went low. A man like George could make ten dollars a day easy. Ten dollars a day, free and clear, every day of
the week, and just for walking up and down the sidewalk
singing songs. That was good steady work.

Climbing over the fence in front of the Elkin mausoleum,
he thought he heard the harmonica. A mockingbird cut a
shrill whistle over the valley and somewhere beyond that a
crow cawed. Then the harmonica again, random notes so
faint they faded away in the wind shift. Or maybe it was only
the wind in the leaves along the ridge. His ears were still
good, he knew that. But it was hard to tell. He struck out
across the graveyard, heading for the terraces above the
camp. He wouldn't go any closer than that. George would be
easy enough to see from there.

The old man hit the carriage path below the Dannenberg
tomb and turned down the hill, and as he passed the obelisk
that said PIERCE, someone called his name. He turned to his
right and saw O'Brien stretched out on the grassy corner of
a terrace, back against a gravestone. He had a slouch hat
pulled down over his eyes and a jackknife in his hand.

"A good day to you," O'Brien said.

The old man ran his hands into his pockets. He fingered
the balls of paper money, the change from his ten. "I got no
truck with you."

"And what kind of a neighbor is this?" O'Brien threw up
his right and waved him over. "Pull up a minute and have a
word."

The old man shook his head. "I don't need none of that.
I'm looking for George, that's all."

"Well, it's not much of a neighbor you are. I can tell ya
that."

The old man fingered the bills in his pocket. "You ain't seen George around, have you?"

"And it's not much of a neighbor you been lately neither. That's what they're saying, ya know. Not since that Kenny boy left us."

"How 'bout George? You seen George today?"

O'Brien wiped the knife blade on his trousers. "Not since last night at Brodsky's Saloon." He dabbed his thumb along the edge of the blade and snickered through his whiskers. "And guess who else I saw down there. It was that Bill Varne. 'Let me find that mangy Pop Ledford,' he says, 'and I'll bust a fucking head. Spread rumors on me, will he?'"

The old man shifted his weight and sized O'Brien out of the corner of his eye. He saw the mouth harp sticking out of his vest pocket. "I ain't spreading no rumors on him. He ain't got no beef with me."

"Says you been making accusations, he does. Says you been saying around he done that Kenny boy in, stuffed his britches with rocks and throwed him in the river, when all the time he just took off on the trains. Says if anybody done him, it was probably you, and you trying now to push off the blame on a guiltless man."

"I ain't said nothing on him. Where'd you get that mouth harp there?"

"What? This one?" O'Brien tapped his pocket with the blade of his knife. "Why, I bought it not a week ago down at Sullivan's. Fifty cents. Lucky buy, wouldn't ya say?"

"Looks like Kenny's, I guess."

"Maybe not. It's a lotta harmonicas in the world, neighbor." O'Brien looked at the sky and scratched the whiskers on his chin. "Or maybe it *is* the boy's, maybe you pawned it down there, eh? You or that Billy Varne, who's to say now?"

"I ain't pawned nothing, I guess. And maybe you didn't buy it down there neither." The old man started backing down the carriage path along the ridge to the river.

"I wouldn't be spreading no more rumors if I was you."
O'Brien folded up the jackknife. "I bought this harmonica at
Sullivan's. Whatever happened to your Kenny boy, I don't
know or care. I'll tell you something about Billy Varne too. I
wouldn't be spreading no more rumors on him neither. He's
got an eye out for you. And if I was you, neighbor, I'd be
pushing on. Billy's a nasty one to be spreading rumors on."

7

CONNIE SAT at the traffic light on College Street, looking across Riverside Drive at the Oak Ridge entrance to the cemetery. In the daylight it wasn't nearly as interesting or eerie — just a narrow concrete road leading downhill to a cream-colored brick gate barred with wrought iron. The main entrance to the cemetery was on a hill off to his right. He couldn't see that gate from where he sat, only the foot of the hill, which was covered with thick beds of red flowers, though they didn't look much like roses.

He had meant to drive through to look for a drop spot that might suit Carl, but it was already eleven o'clock. He'd gone downtown to Thorpe's to buy him a new shirt, then out to the coin laundry on Montpelier. The dryers weren't worth a damn, and drying the underwear and the shirt had taken longer than he'd figured. Carl was going to be pissed enough already, and it was another twenty-three miles down Riverside to the fish camp on Rum Creek. He probably wouldn't get there before eleven-thirty.

The thought of facing Carl made him shiver. But at least he had the shirt. True, buying and washing it had taken too long, but it was better than showing up without it. Carl was still going to be pissed off. There was no way around that. But there was nothing for Connie to do now but let him blow off some steam. He should've gotten back out there last night. He shouldn't have given the shirt to the old man. Then again, Carl knew where he was, and if he'd really been worried he could have driven up to the bait store and phoned. And he could've called any time of the night. It wouldn't have mattered. There was a booth right out there by the ice machine. It might have taken him ten or fifteen minutes at the most. The kid wasn't going anywhere, that was for sure.

Pissing Carl off was bad enough, but now he'd pissed Rita off too. He remembered the look she'd given him as he walked out the door. Rita and Carl, they just didn't mix. And the toughest part was that a lot of the things she said about Carl were true. Only she didn't understand how other things could matter just as much or more. Sure, maybe Carl pushed him around a little when he was a kid, but nobody else did. Nobody even laid a finger on him. Not when Carl was there, anyway. And if he still got a little pissed off now and then, it was generally for a pretty good reason. Rita just thought that everything always had to be hugs and kisses. Always hugs and kisses, sugar and spice. Well, that's just not the way the real world works. He wished now that he'd thought to tell her that. Hugs and kisses, that's just not the way it always works. It was like the old man said, folks are a real mix. And not just bad and good people, but bad and good mixed up in people, mixed up in everybody.

The light changed and Connie took a left onto Riverside. Rose Hill Cemetery fell behind him on his right, then he passed between the stone-covered hills of Riverside Cemetery and crossed the bridge over the interstate. The air was heavy with the sweet stench of the paper mill, but it was too hot to roll up the window. The underarms and back of his T-shirt were already soaked with sweat.

The old bum, or someone who looked like him, was walking on the right-hand shoulder of the road a few hundred feet beyond the end of the bridge. His hands were in his pockets and he leaned forward as he walked, eyes to the ground, watching where he stepped. Connie slowed as he came on him — yes, it was the bum, the shoulder of the new shirt already stained with clay — but he didn't stop. He blew the horn twice and looked into the rearview mirror. The old man didn't notice. Maybe he was walking down to the Waffle House for another burger. Connie smiled when he pictured the old guy flashing the bill in William's face. Two burgers all the way, hash browns, coffee. And a glass of milk.

On his left, Connie passed the Best Western and Howard Johnson's. In one of the rooms at Howard Johnson's, the kid's mother was probably waiting by the phone. He tried to imagine a middle-age woman sitting in her nightgown, watching TV, maybe having her first drink of the day. He wondered what it was like to answer the phone and hear a stranger say he'd snatched your kid. And what was it like now waiting in a motel room in a town you'd never thought about twice in your whole life, waiting by the phone and wondering if you'd ever see your kid alive again, whether you paid the money or not? He guessed she was pouring that drink good and strong.

He gunned it a little to make the yellow light and cruised past the S & S Cafeteria and the Waffle House. As he passed the Gulf station at the edge of the strip, he looked down at his gas gauge. It was almost on empty, but it would get him out to the fish camp and back. Besides, after the shirt and the underwear and the laundry, he had only sixty or seventy cents and the coin the old man had given him. What gas he had would get him to the camp, then he could borrow some money from Carl.

In this whole business the fish camp was Carl's smartest idea. It was an abandoned lodge from the thirties, and Connie imagined it must have been pretty nice in its day — a two-story log house with seven or eight boat ramps, a couple of stone barbecue pits, and a little arbor with a tin roof. The place belonged to a poker friend of Carl's who had bought it from a marijuana farmer in Jones County. It wasn't much good for anything now. One end of the lodge had been caved in years ago by a falling tree that still lay there rotting into the roof. Only a couple of rooms would keep you dry in a strong rain, and all the timbers were a little shaky. Carl had used it before when he needed to get lost for a few days. If you weren't much concerned with comfort, it was still good for that. Actually, it was very good for that. It sat in a wooded bend of the Ocmulgee at the end of three miles of overgrown, washed-out, and nearly impassable dirt road.

At the end of the road, the woods choking out the sky opened into a dusty little clearing — two acres of dirt and scrub brush shaded by five or six huge oaks. In the back of the clearing the lodge sat at a slight angle, within fifty yards of the tracks and the river curving around it. The arbor and the docks were fifty yards off to the right.

Connie eased the Volkswagen out of the woods, over a shallow dip, and into the clearing. Carl's black Cutlass was still parked under the trees on the right side of the lodge. He steered toward it and saw his brother standing behind the wavy glass of an upstairs window. Carl didn't smile or wave, only stood there looking a little odd, a little off-balance with the one naked arm hanging out of his shirt. He didn't look happy.

Connie pulled the Volkswagen beside the Cutlass, got the clothes out of the back seat, and started toward the door. It was noticeably cooler in the clearing, a good breeze coming off the river. He stood for a second in the shade of the oaks and let the breeze crawl under his shirt. Upstairs was already a furnace. He knew that. He looked back up at the window. The glass was splotched with the shadows of the oaks. Carl had moved.

Connie climbed the steps and crossed the porch. It would've

been cooler to have kept the kid downstairs — the kitchen was still in fairly good shape. But Carl had a thing about being higher, about being able to look through the upstairs window and see anybody coming. It didn't matter that there was really nothing to see — the dirt clearing and the pine woods in front of the lodge, the woods, the tracks, and the river behind. And if anybody does come, Connie told him, we could get away a lot quicker from downstairs. But it was Carl's show.

The front door was open, leaning back on one hinge. Connie stepped through the doorway and started up the stairs, trying to make as little noise as possible. The stairs were quiet and solid — thick oak logs split and nailed between heavy beams. Halfway up he stopped. They were talking, but he couldn't make out what they were saying. The boy said something to Carl, and Carl said something back. His voice was tired, but there didn't seem to be any anger in it. It was calm, almost soothing. Connie took a breath and walked on up the stairs.

On the landing, he stood for a second outside the door, trying to hear what his brother was saying, then he stepped into the doorway. Carl was standing beside the table, his hands in his pockets. His hair was mussed and his sweaty shirt stuck to his back in dark blue spots. The kid sat on the mattress, his legs crossed under him. Both of his eyes were black, and his lip was swollen. He was still chained to the radiator.

Connie spread his legs to brace himself. "I got your shirt here."

Carl turned and eyed him standing in the doorway. He tilted his head a little to the right.

Connie stepped a few feet inside the door, but he didn't feel like moving any closer. "I'm sorry about last night, Carl. I was too beat, I guess. I laid down on Rita's bed and I was gone. I didn't wake up till an hour ago."

Carl's face was flushed and sweaty. He shook his head,

looked over at the boy, then back at Connie. "You're a real fuckup, Connie."

"What?"

A peeved smile appeared. "You're a real fuckup, Connie. In fact, you're about the worst fuckup I ever seen."

"No, I ain't. I was goddamn beat, I fell asleep."

Carl's fist slammed into the tabletop. An empty beer can jarred over. "You're a goddamn fuckup. I used to think you were just lazy, but you're a fuckup! You can't do nothing right!" He pointed his finger at Connie. "And don't you say one goddamn word to the contrary."

"I ain't —"

"Shut up, goddamnit!" Carl grabbed a flashlight off the table and threw it at him. It stuck in the wallboard, half in and half out of the wall.

"What the hell?" Connie said. "I fell asleep, big deal! What the hell's wrong with you?"

Carl staggered back a step, then got his balance. He snatched the wine bottle by the neck and cocked his arm. "I ought to break this over your fucking head. Maybe it'd knock some sense into you." The veins stood out in his forehead, sweat beading on his face and neck. The wine bottle quivered in his fist.

"Shit, Carl, calm down. Okay?"

"Don't you tell me to calm down! Don't you ever fucking tell me to calm down!" He turned to his right and threw the bottle through the double panes of the open window. Glass shattered all over Connie's mattress.

"Shit," the boy said.

"Don't you ever tell me to calm down! Not a fuckup like you!"

"Goddamn, Carl. You knew where I was."

Carl shook a fist at him. "What'd I tell you, fuckup?"

"You knew right where I was. You could've gone up to the bait store and called me."

Carl's face flushed deeper, his nostrils flared. He lunged across the room and punched Connie hard in the mouth.

Connie slumped against the wall. He reached up and wiped the blood from his lip. "Goddamn, Carl! You could've —"

Carl punched him again, hard, and Connie slid to the floor.

"Shit!" the boy screamed. "Hit him back!"

Carl spun around and pointed a finger. "Okay, Billy Idol, you want in on this? I'll be right over there."

"Fuck you, asshole!" The boy put his hands over his face and started to cry. "Fuck you, fuck —"

"Shut up!" Carl yelled. "Just shut up!"

"All right," Connie said. "All right, I fucked up."

Carl turned back to Connie. "What'd you say?" He leaned down over him, his fist balled again.

"I said I fucked up."

"You what?"

"I fucked up."

"I guess you did, didn't you?" He took three or four breaths and glared down at Connie. "I guess you really did. Now what the fuck are you gonna do about it?"

Connie looked up at him from the floor. The veins throbbed in Carl's temples, his nostrils flared, his lips tightened to a snarl. "I don't know," Connie said. "Do better, I guess."

"Do better at what?"

"What you tell me, I guess."

Carl kicked him hard on the bottom of his shoe. "You fucking guess?"

"I know."

"You know what?"

"I'm gonna do better."

Carl leaned down over him, almost in his face. "How you gonna do better when you're such a fuckup?"

Connie looked away from him. The shirt and the underwear lay on the floor beside him. He looked at the kid, his knees drawn up under his chin, his arms wrapped around his ankles. "I don't know," he said. "I guess I'll have to figure it out."

Carl straightened up and pushed the hair out of his face. He brushed his eyebrows with the palm of his hand. "I guess you will, won't you? Otherwise, I'm gonna knock your ugly face in." He checked the bandage on his arm, then walked over and sat down in the chair by the table.

Connie sat on the floor. The kid went on crying, quietly now, trying to get hold of himself, but when he looked up and saw Connie watching, he stopped and wiped his eyes. He leaned back against the wall and stared out the shattered window. Connie thought it was strange the way he didn't try to hide his nakedness. For a few hours after Carl had taken his clothes, he'd tried to curl up, hide his cock and balls. But only for a few hours. It was probably just too much effort, and senseless. Connie looked at him now as he leaned into the corner, his hands folded over the black hairs of his crotch. Seeing that hair with his platinum hair was a little odd and disturbing, like finding out an embarrassing secret. And his white skin made it all the worse. Connie thought it looked too soft, too much like a girl's, not a hair on his face, not a hair on his chest or legs. He wished Carl hadn't stripped him. That was a weird thing to do. Nobody was going anywhere. But that was Carl, his temper, his anger.

Connie watched his brother staring out the broken window, his face still flushed and sweaty. He reached across the floor, picked up the blue shirt, and brushed it off. He pushed himself up, stepped over, and laid the shirt on the edge of the table. "It's clean," he said. "I washed it."

Carl glanced at the blue shirt. "You don't remember me telling you twelve o'clock?"

"I fell asleep. I hit the bed and I was gone."

"And you don't remember me telling you twelve o'clock?"

"Yeah, I guess I remember."

"You guess, Connie?"

He shrugged his shoulders. "Yeah, okay. I remember."

"You fucked up, didn't you?"

"I already said that."

Carl stared at him for a second. "In a couple of hours I gotta drive up and call his old lady. I didn't know what the fuck happened to you. Maybe you got picked up by the cops or something. I didn't sleep a wink." He shook his head and took another breath, as though he knew he needed to calm down now and get a grip on things. "I'm sitting over here trying to figure out whether to leave this punk and split or what." He shook his head again. "You're a fuckup, Connie."

"I fell asleep. Anybody can fall asleep."

"Anybody didn't, asshole. You did. You got drunk, didn't you?"

"No, Carl. Honest. Not even a beer."

"Don't lie to me. I hate it when you lie to me. I hate the fuck outta that. You got drunk, didn't you?"

"I ain't lying, Carl. I swear."

Carl held his finger straight up in the air. He pointed toward the wall above Connie's mattress. "If I go down there and find any beer cans in your car, I'll beat the shit outta you, you know that?"

"Carl, I'm telling you the truth."

"I hate you lying to me. I ain't taking that."

"Shit, Carl, I'm telling you the fucking truth."

"If I find out you're not, I'll beat the shit right outta you. You know that, don't you?" He balled his fist and let it fall against his leg. "I swear, fuckup, I'll beat the living shit right outta you."

"You're both fuckups," the boy said, quietly, almost under his breath. "Real fuckups. Nobody ever gets away with stuff like this. You don't let me go, they'll fucking fry you."

Carl raised his fist and let it fall again. "That's cute, kid, but it's really dumb."

"I hope they fry you," the kid said again. "I hope they fucking deep-fry both of you."

"Well, if they do," Carl said, "you won't be around to enjoy it."

The boy didn't say anything. He clenched his teeth and stared back out the broken window.

"What'd you have to hit him for?" Connie said.

Carl's expression went hard again. "Hit him?" He turned back to the boy. "Hey, Billy Idol, I didn't hit you, did I?"

"No, he didn't hit me." He touched his face, the bruises under his eyes, his swollen lip. "This was just a little foreplay. I think the big dude's got tendencies."

"Go ahead, punk," Carl said. "Get smart again."

Connie leaned down over his brother. "I don't like hitting him. It gives me a bad feeling."

"Fuck your feelings. He got a little smart. What could I do?"

"I'm serious. I don't like hitting him."

"So don't hit him." Carl stood up and unbuttoned his shirt. He took it off, wadded it, and wiped his face and chest. He tossed the old shirt into the corner and slipped into the new one.

"I mean it," Connie said. "It gives me a bad feeling."

"You ain't got any balls, you know that?"

"It ain't got nothing to do with balls."

Carl shook his head and went to work on the new shirt, his right hand pushing the buttons into the holes, his left fumbling to pull them through.

Watching the stiff elbow, Connie wondered how he'd blackened both the kid's eyes. "So how's that arm?"

"How you think?"

"I don't know. I ain't never been stabbed before."

"It's sore. That's how it is."

Connie let it slide. He knelt down and started picking up the glass from his mattress. "This cop was asking about you last night."

Carl froze. "Yeah, where was this?"

"Over at the Waffle House. I went in there to get Rita's keys. He wanted to know if I'd seen you?"

"And what'd you tell him?"

"Not since the fight. Just like you told me."

Carl nodded. "You know who it was?"

"Never seen him."

"Wasn't Hancock, was it? The cop that hangs out at the gym?"

"Naw, it wasn't him. He just said to have you call Tommy, that's all."

"You didn't say nothing to nobody else? Nothing to Rita?"

"Shit, no. I didn't say a word."

Carl jabbed his shirttail into his pants, holding his left arm away from his body, trying not to bend the elbow. "Good. But you gotta keep your mouth shut. This ain't no time to fuck up. Another day or two and we're outta here." He folded the sleeves up a few inches above his wrists and sat back down in the chair.

Connie pricked a finger. He held it up to the window and pulled out a tiny sliver of glass. "I found us a place, a good place."

"What kinda place?"

"For the drop. Rose Hill. It's perfect."

"We already got a place."

"Naw," Connie said. "This is a lot better. I was down there last night. You can hide out in there and see everything that goes on. It's just about perfect. Lots of ways to get out, too."

"What were you doing spooking around the fucking grave-yard?"

"I went by and decided to check it out. Looked like just the kinda place we're looking for." He reached up to the window and tossed out a handful of glass. It rattled in the bushes. "There's a thousand places to hide in there. You can see the whole thing, and can't nobody see you."

"We already got a place."

"Yeah? And there might be somebody in the park. There won't be nobody in the graveyard. Nobody that counts, anyway." Connie turned. "And another thing. I don't think they hardly ever patrol Rose Hill, and they drive by Tattnall Square all the goddamn time."

"I'll think about it."

"That's what bothers me," Connie said. "How you know she ain't called the cops? How you know they won't be waiting wherever we tell her to drop the money?"

"She ain't called any cops. I can tell from her voice. She just wants her little punker back. The money don't mean anything to her."

"I don't know. She seems like a pretty smart one."

"You let me worry about that. You just do what I tell you to do, and I'll worry about her."

"Worry all you want," the kid said, "but you're fucked. She's way too smart for you."

Carl smiled at him. "That face don't hurt enough? You don't shut up, you're gonna be the one that's fucked."

"So when you gonna call her?" Connie said.

"A couple of hours, maybe." Carl rubbed his eyes with the heel of his palm. "She's sitting over there in that motel room, sweating in her panties. Let her sweat a while longer. The more she sweats, the better off we are."

Connie tossed more glass out the window. He stood up, turned the mattress on its side and kicked it a few times. What was left sprinkled onto the floor. He shoved the mattress back against the wall. "You know what you oughta do?" he said. "When you call his old lady, you oughta go somewhere and take a cool shower. You'd feel a hell of a lot better."

"And where am I supposed to take a shower?"

"Drive over to Gray and check into that little motel. Take a cool shower and rest for a while."

"That really curls my shit, you know that? You telling me

something like that." Carl shook his head. He looked over at the boy, then back at Connie.

"What the shit?" Connie said.

"Like I could leave you alone for a second with the punk, fuckup, that's what. That really curls my shit."

"What can happen? He's handcuffed to the goddamn radiator, you know he ain't going nowhere."

Carl picked up a beer can and nailed Connie in the chest. "What can happen is you can fuck something else up. That's what can happen, Connie. You can fuck something else up. Hey, look at me. Right here in the eyes. Did you get drunk last night?"

"I told you that already."

"Yeah, you told me all right."

"Then how come you don't drop it, huh? How come you always —"

"Hush." Carl held his hand in the air and turned toward the door. "You hear something?"

Connie listened. "No."

Carl watched the door and felt for his jacket, draped over the back of the chair. He reached into the pocket, came out with a snub-nosed pistol, and hid it low in his lap. He motioned toward the front window.

Connie stepped over and looked out at the yard. Only the two cars and the clearing and the woods beyond. He shook his head and listened. The wind in the tops of the oaks, a crow in the near woods. He stepped across the room to look out the back window. Then he heard it, the light scuff of footsteps. Someone was walking up the stairs.

8

"WELL, MY GOODNESS," the man said as he leaned into the doorway. "Look what we got here. Mr. Carlton and Mr. Connell Holtzclaw, I do believe." He walked into the room, casually, hands in his pockets. Three other men walked in behind him.

Carl's face turned bone gray. "Shit, you about scared me to death, you know that? I didn't know who was coming up those stairs." He laid the pistol on the table, stepped over, and held out his hand.

Tommy smiled at him but kept both hands in his pockets.

Connie had only seen Tommy Wilson a few times, mostly at the fights, and remembered him as a younger and much bigger man. He was stocky but only of average height, and his thin gray hair was slicked back from his forehead. He had on a short-sleeve white shirt, open at the neck, and a pair of wrinkled gray slacks.

One of the men walked over and picked up the pistol. He reached behind his back and tucked it under his belt.

"Sammy's right big on gun control," Tommy said. "So much crime in the streets." He pulled a red bandanna out of his back pocket, took off his glasses, and wiped the lenses. When he put them back on, he looked into the corner at the boy sitting on the mattress. "My goodness, looks like we might've come on a situation here."

"Just a little one," Carl said, trying to smile.

"Maybe a little birthday party," Tommy said. "Looks like he's wearing his suit."

Two of the men chuckled, but not the one who'd taken Carl's pistol.

"Carl, you and Connie might remember my associates here, Mr. Mays and Mr. Arnold." Tommy tossed a thumb at the chucklers. They were big men, over six feet tall and muscular, and both wore red golf shirts. Mays was dark, his face pocked with acne scars, and Arnold was blond, a little stouter, a neck like a log. Connie had seen him a few times at the health club, working out on the Nautilus and the weights.

Carl nodded.

Tommy wiped his mouth with the bandanna. "And I know you remember Mr. Pinyon here. I believe y'all had a little run-in at a card game a while back." The man who'd picked up the pistol was a little older and not quite as toned — gray streaks in his beard, a slight gut hanging over his belt.

"We had a little misunderstanding, that's all."

"Well, misunderstandings can be troublesome things. For instance, some folks might think you been trying to avoid me, that maybe you been trying to welsh on a debt. But me, hell, that never even crossed my mind. I figure we must've just had a little misunderstanding."

Carl held both hands open-palmed in the air. "Tommy, I swear I was just about to call you. I been getting the money together, and I was just about to give you a call."

Tommy wiped his neck with the bandanna. He smiled again. "Well, you see now, that's great. We cleared something up already. We all just misunderstood. And now that we've got together here and talked about it, we've already cleared something up. Now that's swell. That's just the way business-men ought to do things."

Connie eyed the two men on Tommy's right. The taller and darker one, the one called Mays, was watching Carl. He turned slightly to the side, and Connie noticed a pistol wedged under his belt. He couldn't see if the weight lifter had one too.

"And you see," Tommy said, "that makes me feel real good. 'Cause now I know where you're coming from. Now I understand you." He nodded slightly to the man called Pinyon.

Pinyon smiled, stepped over, and hit Carl hard in the stomach. Carl bent double and went down on one knee. Connie started for his brother, but stopped when Mays came out with his pistol.

"What I got to do now," Tommy said, "is make sure you understand me."

"Get up," Pinyon said.

Carl got to his feet and straightened up. He held up his hands and looked over at Tommy. "Tommy," he said, "this really ain't necessary. I —"

Pinyon hit him again, hard, in the stomach. Carl went down on both knees, doubled over, gasping for breath. Pinyon glanced at Tommy, then he kicked Carl in the face and Carl fell onto his side, bleeding from his nose and mouth.

"Okay," Carl said.

"Kick him again," the boy said. "The shitass."

Tommy stared into the corner. The boy was leaning back against the wall, his knees pulled up under his chin. "No, gentlemen," Tommy said, "this doesn't look too good here. I believe we might've stumbled on a real situation." He took a few steps toward the center of the room and gave the boy a closer look. He leaned down over Carl. "I hope this is something easy, Carl. A practical joke, some kinda fraternity thing."

Carl didn't say anything, only lay curled up on the floor, trying to get his breath.

"'Cause if it ain't, Carl, this boy better be a werewolf and it better be a full moon." Tommy stood up and rocked back on his heels. He glanced at Connie, then stared down at Carl. "I really do hope this is something easy, Carl. Something simple."

Carl rolled over onto his back and stared at the ceiling.

Blood still oozed from his nose. "I had to get your money, didn't I? You wanted me to get your money?"

"So you snatched a kid, huh?" Tommy looked around the room and smiled. He coughed, then cleared his throat. "You needed a little money, so you snatched a kid. Pretty easy, huh?"

"Easy enough."

Tommy's face hardened. "Well, shit, why didn't you snatch four or five more and we could've started a baseball team?" He wiped his forehead with the bandanna and stuffed it into his back pocket. "You shithead, you know what kinda problems this causes me?"

Connie looked at the man holding the pistol. He wasn't pointing it at anyone, just holding it in his hand, barrel pointed at the floor. The weight lifter only stood there with his bulging arms folded across his chest. Connie wanted to do something, say something, but he was too scared. The man with the pistol focused on him again, and Connie cut his eyes away, toward the kid on the mattress and then back down at his brother.

Carl pushed himself onto his elbows. The front of his new shirt was covered with blood and there was a small pool drying on the floor. He wiped his mouth and nose carefully on the fold of his sleeve. "I ain't caused you any problems."

Tommy took a breath. He ran his hands into his pockets. "Well, then I guess we don't really understand each other yet."

Pinyon stepped over and kicked Carl hard in the ribs, and Carl went face down on the floor. He pushed his head up a few inches, then went down again on his right cheek.

"That's enough!" Connie said.

Tommy turned. He tugged at his belt. "It is, huh?"

Connie felt something go sour in his stomach.

"Hey," Tommy said. "You used to be a bug man, right? What was it, Orkin or what?"

Connie didn't say anything.

Tommy smiled again. "Hey, you know the best way to kill a bug? Real simple." He stepped over to Carl, lifted the heel of his right shoe, and eased it down on Carl's nose.

Carl jerked his head back, and Pinyon kicked him hard again in the ribs. "Hold still," he said. "Tommy's trying to show us something." He put his boot on the back of Carl's neck and pinned his face to the floor.

Tommy lifted his heel again and eased it down on Carl's nose. He looked over at Connie. "Now the best way to kill a bug, asshole, is to squash it."

Carl's face went red. He yelled, grabbed Tommy's leg with his left hand.

"Don't you do that, shitass." Pinyon banged his heel into the back of Carl's head.

"You know, Carl," Tommy said, stepping back a few feet, "you look a whole lot better like that. Maybe we oughta just change your name to Rudolph."

Pinyon smiled and kicked him again in the ribs.

Carl grabbed his side and rolled over. He lay there for a second, bleeding from his nose, breathing hard. "That's enough," he said. "Let's just get this mess straightened out."

"Straightened out?" Tommy raised his eyebrows. "Well, that's about the smartest thing I believe I've heard all day. Let's do that, why don't we. Let's get this mess straightened out."

Connie watched his brother push to his knees and pause for a minute, still struggling to breathe. His upper lip was busted and his nose was red, the left side scuffed raw. But the bridge of his nose looked worse. It was swollen into a red knot, broken in a way he'd never seen in the ring. Connie felt a new anger rising in him, and he noticed that his hands were shaking. He made two fists and folded his arms.

Tommy stepped over to the back window, slipped his hands into his pockets, and jingled his change. "The way I see it is this," he said. "Mr. Holtzclaw has got us into a real mess here. Looks like he's implicated us in a kidnapping. A felony, a first-class felony." He nodded, staring out the window. "Yes, sir, I believe this just about changes things entirely. That's something, ain't it? A man tries to run down an honest debt, and he finds himself in the middle of a snatching. Yes, sir, this just about changes everything."

"How'd you find this place?" Carl said.

Tommy ignored him, only stared out over the woods and the bend of the river.

"Come on, how'd you guys find us?"

The man with the pistol nodded toward Connie. "You don't want folks to find you, you don't let your brother drive an orange car."

Tommy turned around. A hard expression had come over his face again. "I can't believe this," he said. "You know what the penalty for kidnapping is?"

Nobody said anything.

"Jesus, I just can't believe this," Tommy said, his voice starting to rise. "One phone call and I wouldn't have to chase you all over the goddamn county. One little phone call and I wouldn't be here in the middle of a goddamn snatching." He jerked the bandanna out of his pocket. "I don't know about this business. I got to think about this for a minute." He gazed out the window and wiped his face and neck. "This is a hot place, Carl. And I don't like it when I have to sweat."

Tommy stood quietly for a minute, watching the river, then he walked around the table and leaned over the mattress. "So what's your name, son?"

The boy looked up. "Max."

"You got a last name, Mr. Max?"

"Sheely."

"Okay, Max Sheely, you live around here?"

"I go to Mercer."

Tommy shook his head. "Amazing. He snatched a college boy."

"He's from Jacksonville," Carl said. "His old lady owns about half the fucking town."

"His old lady?"

"His mother. She's into real estate and all kinds of shit. Owns half the fucking town easy."

"Listen," the boy said. "I know if you let me go she'll make it worth your while. We can just forget all this, like it never even happened. She's like that. She'll do it."

"Well, I'm sure she will, son. I'm sure she will." Tommy ran the bandanna between his fingers. "Jesus, Carl, I just can't believe this. You snatched a kid from Mercer?"

"Listen, his old lady's loaded. It's the holidays, nobody else even knows he's missing."

"What about his old man?"

"Dead."

Tommy turned to the man holding the pistol. "Anything about this on the police band?"

"No, but they wouldn't be running nothing like this."

"How 'bout downtown?"

"I ain't heard nothing."

"Well," Tommy said. "This might still be a fairly clean job." He dug a pack of Winstons and a Bic lighter from his shirt pocket.

"Could I have one of those?" the boy said. "The asshole won't let me smoke. Thinks I'll burn the place down."

Carl was still on his knees in the center of the room.

"You think he's gonna burn the house down when he's shackled to the goddamn wall?" Tommy gave the boy a cigarette and lit it for him. Then he put his hand under the boy's chin and tilted it toward him. "Looks like somebody's been doing some pretty strong talking."

"He's a tough guy," the boy said.

"Yeah, I see how tough he is." Tommy lit his own cigarette. "How come you're such a tough guy, Carl?"

"I ain't a tough guy. You know that." He had rolled up his sleeve and was checking his bandage.

Tommy tossed the pack of cigarettes and lighter onto the mattress and walked over to the back window. He leaned out and spit, then turned and gave Carl a smile. "What happened to your arm, Carl? He bite it?"

Carl sat back on his heels. "Sort of."

"Sort of? What does that mean?"

"He stabbed me with a fucking pocket knife."

Tommy dabbed the bandanna around his hairline, wadded it, and pushed it back into his pocket. "And I suppose you gave him the knife to cut his toenails?"

"Connie left it on the table. I thought the kid could sit over there in the corner and behave himself." A trickle of blood ran into his mouth. He wiped it with his right sleeve.

"Looks like you fucked up, don't it?"

"I fucked up before."

Tommy nodded in thought. "I don't guess anybody here would argue about that, Carl. But the question here is, what do we do about your fuckups? The way I see it, I got two choices. The first one is simple. I can just turn you and your brother over and be clean of this shit." He flipped his ashes onto the floor and observed Carl's face. "But then maybe I don't get my eight thousand dollars. They might just send you away for a pretty long time. Maybe a lot longer than I'd wanna wait on my money. Eight thousand dollars is a bunch of money to get cheated out of, Carl. And times are sort of tough right now. The city just closed down two of my bookstores. I'm gonna drop a bunch on lawyers, Carl. No, eight thousand's more than I might wanna lose."

Tommy glanced back out the window, then over at the boy. He turned and stepped toward Carl. "The only other choice I got is to hang around here and make sure this thing gets handled the right way. Make sure things run smooth and all the loose ends get tied up. But, then, that involves a considerable risk, doesn't it? And I'm not sure eight thousand dollars is quite enough money to cover a risk like that. You following me, Carl? You hear what I'm saying?"

Carl nodded.

"Now this Ms. Sheely, who you say owns half of Jacksonville, you got in touch with her yet?"

"Yeah."

"And she's agreed to pay for the kid?"

"Two hundred. She's already got it together, and she's in town. Howard Johnson's, on Riverside."

A shock wave went through Connie. He tried to control it, but he felt his face flush. Two hundred? Two hundred was news to him.

"That's a lot of money, Carl." Tommy took a drag off his cigarette. "For one person. But there seems to be more like six of us here." His gaze strayed over the room. "Now two hundred for six of us ain't all that good. I mean, you figure it out, Carl. Considering what the penalty is for kidnapping, that don't really make choice number two all that attractive, now does it?"

Carl didn't answer him. He didn't look up.

Tommy looked across the room at him. "You feeling better, Carl? Why don't you get up and sit down in that chair there?"

Carl sat on his heels for another few seconds. He grabbed the back of the chair and pulled himself to his feet, watching Pinyon out of the corner of his eye. He wiped his lip and sat down in the chair.

"Now, as I was pointing out," Tommy said, "two hundred just don't seem like a lot of money for six people. No, when you stop to think about it, that don't make choice number two real attractive. And choice number two, Carl, is the choice that keeps you and your brother here outta prison."

Carl touched the bridge of his nose.

"I don't know where they'd be liable to send you for something like this. Reidsville, maybe. Hard to say. Anyhow, ain't none of these prisons very nice places anymore, Carl. Prison ain't much fun, you can take my word for it. And now there's all this AIDS shit going around."

Carl didn't say anything.

"No," Tommy said, "choice number two ain't all that attractive. I suppose we could ask Mama for more money, but that might take a little time. And time means risk. And I don't think we need any more of that. No, two hundred for six ain't really very much."

"Two hundred for four's a little better," Carl said.

"Fuck you!" Connie said. "You ain't giving away my goddamn money! You told me it was a goddamn hundred! You told me half. You told me fifty. You fucking liar! You ain't —"

Pinyon sprang across the room and swung a right at Connie's jaw. Connie slipped most of it but staggered back against the wall. He caught himself quick and hit Pinyon flush on the chin with a short right hand, and Pinyon fell back, surprised. Connie started to swing again, but the other two men jumped him, the weight lifter punching him with both fists and Mays slapping him once with the frame of the pistol.

"Okay," Tommy said. "Don't kill him."

Connie lay face down on the floor. His head and ribs felt like they'd been beaten with a hammer. He spit blood and breathed slowly through his mouth. He could feel his lip and left eye swelling. He opened his eyes, and the left filled up with blood. He closed them again and lay still.

"See if he's all right," Tommy said.

Connie heard boot heels jar across the floor. Then the toe of a boot nudged him easy on the chin, wedged under his jaw, and lifted his face. It smelled like leather and polish. "The shitass is fine," Pinyon said. The boot let him fall.

"Get up, Connie," Tommy said. "You ain't hurt bad. I want you to hear all of this."

Connie lay for a minute longer, every breath stabbing a pain through his ribs, then he mustered some strength and pushed himself onto an elbow. He wiped the blood away from his eyes and opened them. The room was a blur. He wiped them again, and things began to clear.

"Good," Tommy said. "If you'd had that much spunk in the ring, you'd been a lot better fighter."

Connie's anger throbbed. He wanted to get up and butcher Tommy, pound his knuckles into Tommy's face. But he only lay there, propped on an elbow. He knew better.

"Now, Carl," Tommy said. "What was it you were saying?"

There was a long silence in the room. Carl sniffed twice to clear his nostrils. "I said two hundred for four's a little better."

"Well, yes it is," Tommy said. "And I'm glad you brought that up. It's not a considerably better proposition, but it is a little bit better." Tommy took a drag on his cigarette, turned, and flipped it out the window. "Then, too, you boys seem to be in a real mess here. And I've never been the kinda man to turn his back on a friend that needed a little help. You know that, don't you, Carl?"

Carl shifted in the chair. "Sure."

Connie pushed himself up and leaned against the wall. He pulled up the tail of his T-shirt and started wiping his face.

"Well, I'd like to help you out," Tommy said. "I'd like to see that this mess gets cleaned up the way it ought to."

"I'd appreciate it," Carl said quietly, almost in a whisper. "I'd appreciate the help."

"Well, what about you, Connie? How do you feel about that?"

Connie studied Carl's face, his broken nose, the blood still trickling from his nose and lip.

Tommy turned back to Carl. "Your brother seems to be a little tongue-tied right now, Carl. How do you think he feels about it?"

"He'd appreciate it," Carl said.

"Well, that's good. I'm glad y'all are in agreement about this. Now that only leaves us with one little problem. And that's my eight thousand dollars. If I do you this little favor, I'm gonna have a few expenses. I got to bring somebody in here to clean this mess up. I don't really like to handle something like this myself. I got to call somebody in, Carl. And that kinda help ain't cheap."

"Sure," Carl said. "I'll get you your money."

Tommy folded his hands behind his back. "Well, that's real good. That'd be real considerate."

"You're a shithead," the boy said, crushing his cigarette into the linoleum. "Just like these other shitheads. You better just let me go."

Tommy looked surprised. "Listen, son, don't play hard with me. I'll make them black eyes look like love pats."

The boy slid back on the mattress and leaned against the wall.

Tommy took out the bandanna again, wiped his forehead and the back of his neck. "All right, Carl, let's clear a couple of things up. How come this particular kid? How'd you find him? How'd you know about his old lady?"

Carl sniffed back the blood. "I saw him a few times in the Rookery. He used to hang around there on the weekends, spend some money. I heard some talk about him. I asked around."

"Yeah? Who'd you ask?"

"Some bartender. I don't remember her name?"

"You make a big deal out of it?"

"No."

"Suppose somebody talked to this bartender. You think she'd remember you asking about him?"

"Hell no. People talk in bars."

Tommy shook his head. "I don't like that, Carl. I don't like any kinda connection at all."

"There ain't no connection," Carl said.

"So how'd you pick him up?"

"Wasn't too hard. He drives an Alfa. I got his tag number,

I started following him around. It was close to the holidays, so I figured he'd be going home. I followed him out to the airport."

"You snatched him in the airport?"

"In the parking lot."

"So where's his car?" Tommy said.

"It's still out there in the parking lot."

"That's good. That's a good place for it. When's he supposed to be back in school?"

"I don't know. Not until next week, anyhow."

Tommy turned to the kid. "When you supposed to be back in school?"

"Fuck you," he said.

"Shit," Tommy said. "Don't start this shit with me." He wiped his hands with the bandanna and stuffed it back into his pocket. "How long you got off? A week? The weekend?"

"Fuck off," the boy said.

Tommy stepped over to the mattress, grabbed the chain, and jerked the kid's hands tight against the radiator. He wrapped the chain twice around the valve handle, reached down, and picked up the Bic.

The boy jerked at the cuffs, but the chain wouldn't give. "Shitass," he said. "You're fucking crazy."

Tommy flicked the lighter.

"Shit," the boy said. "Monday. A goddamn week from Monday."

Tommy snapped it off. "I'm crazy, all right," he said. "You remember that and we'll get along a lot better." He unwound the chain and tossed it to the floor. The boy crawled back against the wall.

Tommy took a breath and dropped the lighter onto the mattress. He nodded at the kid, then walked back over to Carl. "Okay, Carl, a week from Monday. And this Ms. Sheely is over at the Howard Johnson's?"

"That's right."

"And she's got the money?"

"She's got it," Carl said.

"Well, where's she gonna leave it?"

Carl ran his finger easy over the bridge of his nose. He brushed his eyebrows with the palm of his hand. "I'm supposed to call her today and tell her. We figured Tattnall Square or Rose Hill."

Connie felt himself tense again. Carl was going to give the whole thing away. A few bruises and a broken nose, and he was going to sit there and give Tommy Wilson whatever he wanted.

Tommy looked over at Pinyon. "What do you think?"

"The cemetery'd be okay."

Tommy thought about that. "Well, it's close to the motel. Anybody ever nosing around in there?"

"A few people in the daytime," Pinyon said. "Nobody at night."

"Is it a good place?" Tommy said.

"As good a place as I can think of. A cruiser might ride through there once a night. I don't know when, but we can find out. And there's a lot of ways in and out."

Tommy turned back to Carl. "Anyplace special in there that might be a good place to drop it?"

Carl leaned over and spit some blood on the floor. "You got me. The graveyard's Connie's idea."

"What about it, Connie? Anyplace special?"

Connie didn't answer.

"Don't you get silly on me too, kid. An attitude like that could be a real problem."

"Anyplace in there's okay," Pinyon said. "We'll stake it out. Just tell her to park her car across the street and walk through the front gate. Tell her to walk halfway down the hill or so and drop the bag behind a headstone."

"What time?" Tommy said.

"Don't matter. Anytime tonight. Tell her three o'clock or

so. Shouldn't be anybody in there then. I'll check downtown, see if I can find out when the cruiser goes through. If that's a bad time, we'll call her back."

"All right," Tommy said. "Now all we got to do is find somebody to pick the money up."

"Any of us can do that," Pinyon said.

"No, we'll let one of these gentlemen do it." He eyed Carl slouched over in the chair, then Connie leaning against the wall. "And I think it might be little brother. I think his attitude might just straighten out by tonight. And I don't know about Carl here. He might just get a little crazy again." Tommy paused for a second. "Yeah, I think we'll let little brother carry out the bucks. Carl can stay here and keep us company." He turned to Mays and the weight lifter. "Y'all can go with him. Stake the place out, but you let him go down for the money. I don't want nobody else getting picked up down there. And you make damn sure nobody's following him before you let him come back to the car."

"You want us to come back out here?" Mays said.

"No, I don't think so. You go on home, and I'll call you in the morning." He looked the weight lifter. "Robert, you take Carl's wheels and run on back into town. See if you can find Jerry Fry. If he ain't home, check out the bar at the Hilton. Tell him we got something for him. I'll be home in an hour or so. Tell him to call me there. And you stay with him till he calls. You hear that?"

"Sure. And what if he ain't around?"

"He's around somewhere. You turn him up." Tommy thought for a second. "We can't find him though, we'll just have to handle it ourselves."

"I can handle it," Pinyon said.

"I know that," Tommy said. "But we'll look for Fry first." He held out his hand toward Carl. "You got some keys?"

Carl pointed to the table. Tommy picked up the keys and tossed them to the weight lifter. "You stay with him till he calls." Then he turned to Pinyon. "Sammy, go bring the car down, and you and me'll take Carl to make a little phone call."

Connie pushed himself up off the floor and stood beside the window. He took a few deep breaths and looked out over the trees falling down the hill toward the river. He felt the lump under his left eye. It was sore and tight and it felt like it wanted to split open. His mouth hurt and he had a headache. A little blood was still oozing from his lip. He leaned over the window ledge and spit.

"You'll live."

He turned toward Mays, who was sitting in the chair now, the pistol wedged again under his belt. "I been hurt worse than this."

"It ain't nothing to brag about."

"I ain't bragging about it." Connie walked across the room and sat down on the mattress under the front window. He studied Mays's face — the small brown eyes, the pockmarks that looked like they'd been made with an ice pick — then he glanced over at the boy, who was still leaning back against the wall, his hands folded in his lap.

"What're they gonna do with him?" Connie said.

"Don't worry about it. He'll be fine."

"Then what's all this shit about Fry?"

"You worry too much. You'd do a lot better just to sit there and keep your mouth shut. Everything's gonna be fine. Just take a lesson from your boyfriend in the corner."

Connie watched the kid leaning against the wall. His eyes were closed, and Connie wondered what he was thinking. He was a pretty tough kid, he had some guts. He hadn't really gone to pieces. Not like most guys would have. Connie admired that, but a sickness swept through him. Everything wasn't going to be fine. He knew it. First he'd hit the kid, then Carl had tried to cheat him. And now this business about Fry.

He didn't want to be any part of it. He thought about Carl and the money. So that's why Carl was picking up the bag. He was going to skim half off the top before he split the rest. Carl said a hundred, and all along it was going to be two. The sickness turned in Connie's stomach. But that was Carl. He knew better than to lie to Tommy. He knew better than to let Tommy even think he was trying to cheat him. That was Carl, all right. It was all true to form.

He thought about his brother lying on the floor, bleeding from his nose and mouth, and for the first time an odd sense of satisfaction came over him. The horror and the fear were there too, but also now an odd sense of satisfaction, not exactly vengeance, not exactly justice.

"Carl tried to cheat me, you know that? My own fucking brother, and he tried to cheat me."

Mays shrugged. "So what?"

"So he's my goddamn brother, that's what."

Mays smiled. "You kill me, kid."

"Oh yeah?"

"Your brother's a shitass." Mays slipped off his right loafer and propped his foot on his left knee.

"Is that right?" Connie said. "So what's he ever done to you?"

Mays pulled off his sock and examined the foot. "He ain't done nothing to me, and he ain't going to. I just don't like his attitude, that's all." He rubbed the side of his big toe and leaned down to take a closer look. "Shit, I'm getting a bunion." He rubbed the toe and frowned. "Your brother's a pretty boy shitass. That's all I know about him, that's all I gotta know."

A mild shock went through Connie, a recognition, and he knew that what he felt, the odd joy, wasn't just because of the money. It wasn't just because Carl had tried to cheat him, but it was something much deeper, something old that had surfaced again. It was Carl's good looks, his attitude. How many

times had Carl called him a shitface or a turdface or something worse, and he'd felt that same hate sweep through him.
No, not hate, that was too strong. But resentment. For sure,
resentment. He thought again of Carl lying on the floor of
the lodge, the bridge of his nose swollen and red. He didn't
want the picture to be so good, but it was good and he
couldn't deny it. It satisfied something that went back too far.

"A shitass," Mays said again. "It don't take much to see
that."

Then a memory came to him, a memory of a fear. He was
lying in his bed in the house in Montana. He was about six,
his room was dark, and he was still a little bit afraid of the
dark. Through the window he could see the gray drifts of
snow blowing against the house. The window was constantly
spotting with tiny shadows, and the wind brushed the tree
limbs against the roof. It was Christmas Eve, and a noise had
jarred him awake. Not the limbs against the house or the
growl and rattle of the furnace, but a noise outside in the hall.
Someone was outside his room and trying to move quietly,
trying to step softly to keep the floor from creaking. He remembered thinking it was Santa Claus. But what would Santa
be doing out there. Santa? Or maybe a burglar? Yes, that was
the fear. Someone had broken into the house to murder them
in their sleep and steal their presents. The doorknob turned
and the door eased open. It squeaked a little on its hinge,
stopped, and squeaked again. It was too dark to see, but he
didn't want to see. He was too afraid. He held his eyes shut
tight. On his face he could feel the warmth of someone's
breath. The breath hovered over him and didn't move, warm
and slow, hovering over his eyes and nose. He lay rigid in the
bed, listening to the quiet wheeze. "You're so ugly," Carl whispered. "If Santa Claus brings you anything tonight, it's because he feels sorry for you."

"Hey," Mays said. "You hear anything?"

Connie listened for a second. There was only a bird somewhere in the woods behind him. He didn't know what kind. He shook his head.

"I thought I heard something."

He remembered the first time he told that story to Rita, how amazed she was. But he shouldn't tell her things like that, it just fueled the fire. If they could've just gotten to Montana, it wouldn't have made any difference. But now, who knows? It was all slipping away. "I was gonna get outta this shithole," he said. "I was gonna take that money and start something."

Mays pulled on his sock. "You fucked up."

"I didn't fuck up. Carl fucked up. He started all this shit."

"That's right," Mays said, not very interested. "Carl fucked up."

"If he wasn't my brother, I'd kill him."

Mays slipped his foot back into his shoe and crossed his legs. "Why don't you give it a rest, pal? Sit back there and relax. Turn on the radio."

But Connie only slid across the mattress and leaned against the wall. He thought about Rita and Montana, the house and the land he'd promised her. And he wondered why he could never keep a promise to her. Was he like the painter? He thought about the things the painter had told her, the promises he'd made. He thought about Rita lying in the painter's bed, her legs wrapped around his legs. He felt the muscles tense in his face. Was he like the painter? Was he just making promises? Not one thing he'd planned had ever worked out — not one job in a string of jobs, not the boxing. And now this promise to Rita. Did he know all along that he'd never have anything to give her, that somehow this deal would get fucked up just like everything else?

He felt a new anger rising in him. Not an anger at Carl or Tommy Wilson or Tommy's goons, but an anger at himself. When was he going to do something right? When was he going to stop fucking up? Was he going to fail with Rita just like he'd failed at everything else? "Hey," he said, "what you gonna do with your money?"

Mays looked puzzled. "What're you talking about?"

"The money you get outta this. What you gonna do with it?"

"Tommy'll get most of this money. We work for Tommy."

"You'll get some money. What you gonna do with it?"

"How the fuck do I know?"

"You know."

Mays gave him a smile. "Fuck it away, kid. That's what I'm gonna do."

"I ain't surprised," Connie said, disgusted. "You know what I was gonna do? I was gonna start something, buy a little piece of land with my girlfriend. Get a start, you know? Get a start on something permanent."

"You got yourself a girlfriend, huh? So what's her name?"

"Rita Estes."

"Rita Estes?" Mays said. "Sure, cute girl. I fucked her once."

Connie felt his face flush. He sat up on the mattress, both hands balled into fists.

"Relax, kid. It's a joke."

Connie stood up, his face flushed, his fists still balled.

"Relax, kid. It's just a joke."

"I ain't much in the mood for jokes right now."

Mays swung around in his chair. "You gonna be in a lot worse mood if you don't sit back down and try to relax. We gotta wait here anyhow, so we might as well just take it easy."

Connie sat down on the mattress and edged back against the wall. He tried to calm himself by thinking of Rita. He remembered the way she woke him last night, the way she climbed on top of him and eased her body down onto his, the way she moved them like a wave in the room. He loved that best when she did it in candlelight, the little sticks of sandalwood burning on the dresser, the Allman Brothers on the stereo. Rita called that total sensuality. She got that from one of her books, but it seemed right — the light and smell and sound, and the taste of Rita, the touch of her moving their bodies. And he loved waking up with her in the morning, the sun easing through the window to light up the fine blond hairs on her arms. He liked to see the sun in her hair, watch it spark off the five gold rings in her ear. Then he thought again of the painter. The picture of Rita on her knees, the painter in her mouth. The pain of it hit him with a blow that took his breath.

It was a familiar pain, but a pain he'd not known before Rita, something he'd only heard about and seen in other people, something he'd never understood, the sort of pain you saw in movies or read about in magazines. He thought about the first time he discovered that anyone could really hurt that way. A year ago, maybe more, and the whole thing had seemed only a little embarrassing. The phone woke him up about one in the morning. It was Eddie Carano, the promoter who'd booked his next fight, a ten-rounder with Wayne Lester, a journeyman, an easy decision.

Connie was surprised that Eddie was calling so late. "So what can I do for you?" he said.

"What can you do for me?"

"That's right."

"What can you do for me? That's pretty funny."

"Yeah?"

"I hear you been fucking my wife."

Connie was stunned. Okay, but he was only one in a string of fighters. "No, Eddie, I ain't. Where'd you hear something like that?"

"Don't hand me that shit. You been fucking my wife."

Then the shock turned into contempt. He couldn't believe this man was waking him up in the middle of the night and telling him this. "So what're you gonna do about it, Eddie? Come over here and beat me up?"

There was a silence on the line.

"So how 'bout it, Eddie," he said. "You know how to get to my place?"

The phone went dead then, and Connie thought that was the end of it. But when the fight came up, Wayne Lester suddenly caught the flu. There was a last-minute substitution, a kid named Rick Hugo who was ranked number fifteen by the WBC. Connie almost bowed out, but he didn't want anyone saying he ducked Hugo or anybody else. That was important to him. Connie Holtzclaw didn't duck anybody. But Hugo was too strong and wanted to hurt him. Connie remembered almost going down three or four times, but each time Hugo backed off his head, let him recover, and worked his body. By the fifth round he'd broken Connie's nose and closed his left eye, and in the last round he cracked two ribs. What Connie remembered best was the doctor leaning over him in the dressing room, then the ambulance ride to the hospital. He spent two nights there, and after that he didn't want to fight anymore.

Eddie had his ways. Connie thought he'd never be able to forgive him for that. But now he knew that it didn't have anything to do with getting even. It had to do with pain and fear. It had to do with helplessness, desperation, sickness, with loving a woman so much you couldn't imagine a life without her. And Connie knew now that the beating he'd taken from Rick Hugo was nothing like the beating Eddie Carano had taken from his wife, and it was nothing like the beating he might take from Rita.

When the car came into the clearing, Connie turned and looked out the window. It was a yellow Cadillac with a yellow vinyl top, the fenders and sides red with dust. Connie watched it cross the clearing and stop in the shade on the near side of his Volkswagen.

"That Tommy?" Mays said.

Connie nodded. He watched Pinyon get out of the back seat on the driver's side. He had two large grocery bags in his arms. Carl got out of the front on the passenger's side and walked around the car. They stood for a minute, Pinyon leaning into the driver's window, talking to Tommy. Connie stared over the window ledge at the three of them — Tommy in the driver's seat, Pinyon leaning into the window, his arms full of groceries, Carl standing behind him. Carl could have reached right down and lifted the pistol out of Pinyon's belt. No problem at all. He could have reached right down and lifted it out clean. Carl put his hands in his pockets and gazed down toward the river. He was a coward. He wouldn't even look at the pistol. For the first time in his life, Connie thought he really hated his brother.

9

THE OLD MAN WATCHES the moon. All its anger bled away, the moon balances on the tip of a pine like a ball on a juggler's stick. The stars around it are like silver sequins on a black cape. Or better still, the old man thinks, like sequins on a black curtain. Yes, the stars in the sky are like sequins on a black curtain. And what is that curtain hiding? The huge moon is white, all its anger vanished. Now there is only clarity, and cunning. It throws a gold path on the river, and the path leads to a man lying beside a campfire. The night is warm and humid, but the sleeper points his feet toward the fire. Over the river the wind scatters the pine scent, the owls keep asking a question. Off toward town, dogs howl at the moon and their breath stirs the wind above the pinetops. The moon wobbles. Maybe it will fall through the trees and crack like an egg.

In the damp grass of the grave terrace, the old man lies on his belly and observes the sleeper. Varne, the fire dying out at his feet, his snore like the rumbling of freights. Orange in the firelight, a moth circles the flame and the tips of his shoes. Varne, maker of threats, big bully of winos. A circle of stones guards the fire, but the wind makes it dance. Smoke sweeps into the graveyard, and the moth fights the wind. Such great fortune. Billy Varne, alone, in the peace of his dream.

The old man listens to the sound of the river. Somewhere in the black water a voice lies buried. Somewhere in the mud of the bottom, stuck among turtles and stones, tickled by the whiskers of catfish, a tongue wags day and night. Wags but can't speak. But the river itself is a tongue, and the old man listens. Varne's chest rises and falls in the firelight. His long hair is orange in the firelight, and so are the edges of his trousers and shoes. A snore comes off him like the rattle of boxcars. Where is Billy Varne traveling in his dream?

A large rock appears in the old man's hand. A large white rock that catches the moon like marble. He hefts it in the light and studies its angles. Heavy as a sledge, it has sharp points. He drags his thumb across its edges. He turns it to the left and it's almost a skull — two small eye sockets, a chin like an ax.

Varne coughs in his sleep, slaps a bug from his face. The orange moth flutters above the fire. Above the riverbank a bat dips through the shadows. Big man Varne in the peace of his dream. What fool is he cheating at cards? What flophouse tramp is he rolling? The old man hefts the rock as if it were a skull. Its white face catches the moonlight, takes on the warmth of his hand. Its weight is steady and good. Its chin is the blade of an ax.

He inches to the edge of the terrace and studies the drop. The wall is six feet, maybe eight. Varne rests happy in the sin of his dream, his chest a steady rise and fall. The old man lowers a leg over, then the other. He hangs for a moment by an elbow and lets himself down.

Over the hill above him, a single note from a mouth harp. He hesitates. He questions the eyes of the rock, and they show him what to do. But the harp comes again, barely cutting the air, a long faint melody sweeping the graves. The old man thinks he knows the tune. Beautiful notes drifting over the hills. O'Brien? Something isn't right? Kenny? The old man turns and regards the sleeper, whose hands are folded now across his chest. His hair is orange in the firelight. The wind whips the smoke toward the river.

The mouth harp comes over the hill, beautiful and distant, rich as an organ, and the old man steps toward the sleeper. The rock feels good in his hand, but the music is rich and mellow. A harp or an organ? Fire and smoke sway to it. The moth dances queasy circles, and suddenly he sees a small hand fluttering over the page of a hymnal and remembers the words of the song. *I want to meet you by that beautiful river, in that eternal morning in the sky. Where we'll live in peace through endless ages, where we'll never say good-bye.* The moon wobbles, the stars shiver. The rock floats high in the air, high above the head of the sleeper. Then the old man freezes. The face he dreams is no longer Varne's — it's the face of the red-haired woman.

10

WHEN THEY REACHED the wrought-iron fence, Connie grabbed hold of the top rail, swung a leg up, and climbed over. The two men climbed after him, and they stood for a minute looking over the hill of stones and mausoleums. Connie remembered standing in the same spot with the old man, then walking down the carriage path toward the valley. But now the cemetery looked different. The sky had clouded and only a few dim stars shone through in patches. The moon was hidden completely behind the clouds and the dark smudged most of the small stones into the hills.

Mays prodded Connie in the chest with his flashlight. "You fuck with me in here and you're a dead fucker. You know that, don't you?"

Connie nodded.

Mays wedged the flashlight into his left back pocket. "You do exactly what I tell you, kid. And you don't do nothing else." He stood for a second, surveying the hill of dull stones, then turned to the weight lifter. "All right, let's stay real close." He started off toward the trees across the path, walking quickly toward the big mausoleum that said DANNENBERG. Connie followed him, stepping fast to keep up, and the weight lifter followed Connie.

When they reached the mausoleum, they were on top of a

hill that looked down over the center of the graveyard, but most of the valley was hidden. They were still too deep in the trees.

"Down there's a pretty good place," Connie said. He pointed toward a giant oak and the gray obelisk sitting under it. "Lots of cover and you can see the whole valley."

"Where's the main gate?" Mays said.

Connie gestured toward the far hill on his right. A dark bush of trees stood in their way. "You can see it better from down there."

"All right, move it."

Connie walked down through the graves, keeping off the path, and the two men followed. They stopped beside the oak and sat down on a low wall behind the obelisk that said PIERCE.

"Is that the gate up there?" Mays said.

Connie pointed up the hill to their right. "You can see the roof of the office up there. See it?"

"Yeah, I guess."

"The top of the gate is right beside it."

"Which side?" Mays said.

"Left. See it there? She'll walk right through that gate and down the path. When she comes outta those trees, we can see everything she does."

Mays looked out over the hills and the terraces of stones. "You just remember that I better see everything you do."

Connie listened to the crickets in the distance. A truck blew its horn in the street behind him. He weighed what Mays said.

"You just remember that."

"What am I gonna do?"

"I don't know. I just know that dumb runs in your family, kid. And you don't wanna do nothing dumb."

"I ain't Carl," he said. "Carl's the dumb one, Carl's the fool."

"That's good. You don't wanna be Carl. Right now a fool's about the last thing you wanna be."

Out of the darkness to the left, where the creek ran down the gorge toward the river, a few frogs opened up in deep belches. The huge noise was almost startling. Carl a fool? Why did it feel so strange to hear himself say that? But it was true. He knew that now because Carl had given up. From the second he'd seen Tommy Wilson walk through the door of the lodge, he'd given up on everything. Carl was a fool because he was a coward. It washed through Connie with a shivering clarity. And a coward will always think of himself first. That was Carl, all right. You could take that definition and apply it to every day of Carl's life.

"I ain't Carl," Connie said half under his breath.

"That's good," Mays said. "You remember that. The one guy you don't wanna be is Carl."

"What time is it?" the weight lifter said.

Mays pulled the flashlight out of his pocket, shined it on his wrist, and switched it off. "We got a good forty-five minutes." He leaned down and laid the flashlight in the grass between his feet. "You wanna walk around some and check things out?"

The weight lifter tilted his head. "Not especially."

"Well, why don't you do it anyway? Make sure the whole police department ain't over there." He looked down the ridge to his left toward the deep croaking coming out of the gorge, then back up the valley. "Walk down this ridge and circle up the other side. Check out the blind side of that hill over there."

The weight lifter pushed himself up and started walking off through the trees to the left. Connie watched him moving behind the stones, trying to stay inside the tree line, inside the deepest shadows. He was moving off toward the frogs, heading toward the ridge where the old man had left the carriage path and crawled downhill toward the grave. Before long he was lost in the trees and the stones.

"When the bitch drops the bag," Mays said, "Arnold'll make sure she's gone, then you go straight down there, pick it up, and come straight back up this hill. Maybe we won't be here, but we'll be around here somewhere. And we'll be watching every goddamn move you make. Don't you fucking look around like there's somebody up here, you got that?"

"Sure."

"You walk straight out to the car and get in the back seat and sit there. When we're satisfied nobody's following you, we'll all drive home."

A bird whistled off the far hill, a loud warble that moved in waves through the valley. Connie flapped some air under his shirt, and the wind shifted to the north, blew in the stench of the paper mill.

Mays jabbed his finger into Connie's arm. "You don't let me lose sight of you for a goddamn second. You understand what I'm telling you?"

"Sure."

Mays gave him a look. "Not one goddamn second. You stay on these roads here. You step behind one gravestone so I can't see you and that's where you'll stay, pal. You know what that means?"

Connie inched back on the wall. "I think so."

"You better think so, kid. Or that little fuck muffin of yours'll be carting flowers to a place like this."

Connie studied the expression on Mays's face. It had taken on an edge, like the face of someone trying to start a bar fight, someone drunk on meanness and a need for violence. He gazed back into the valley, then down toward the gorge, where the croaking had thinned out but still came on. Two small stars were trying to punch through the clouds over the river. They shone for a second, dim and fuzzy, then the wind plugged the cloud cover. A strong blast from the paper mill washed over the graveyard with the smell of something spoiled. Connie thought of Rita. She was the worst part of all this. He thought of the five tiny rings in her right ear, her car parked all night in the painter's driveway, the pictures in her dresser drawer. An anger rose in him again. "I ain't Carl," he said.

"You remember that."

Connie clenched his jaws. "I intend to."

Off to the left at the end of the valley, the weight lifter came into view. He stopped for a second in a cluster of tall stones, turned, and waved up at the hill where they were sitting.

Mays shook his head. "What the fuck's he doing? Trying to show everybody where we are?"

The weight lifter walked on toward the hill across the valley and started climbing through the stones at the foot of the slope. He climbed all the way across the crest, stopping occasionally to check his back. Connie watched him carefully and noticed something. Whenever he stopped, whenever he stood still, he became very hard to see among the stones. The darkness turned him into a statue.

Turning away from them, the weight lifter melted into the deep shadow of a mausoleum. Connie saw a dim flash of his shirt as he walked behind a tall stone, then another. Then he disappeared.

"What's on the other side of that hill?" Mays said.

Connie remembered asking the old man the same question. What had he said? "More hills, more graves."

An owl hooted twice from the woods across the river, then a third time in a faint echo. Mays leaned down and propped his elbows on his knees. He listened. The pistol was wedged under his belt directly over his right back pocket. If he leaned up a little farther, Connie thought he might be able to grab it. Maybe. But then what? It wasn't as though they were all in the same place. It wasn't like all of them being at the fish camp. Carl and the kid were twenty-three miles away. Besides, the pistol was no good without the money. A pistol shot could ruin everything. Everybody knew that. The money came first. The pistol was for after the money.

"You see him up there anywhere?" Mays said.

"No."

Mays slapped Connie on the shoulder. "You ain't even looking, goddamnit. Pay attention to what the fuck's going on."

Connie turned to the hills and terraces of graves and thought again about the money, about the things it would buy in a place like Montana. It wasn't that he didn't believe Rita cared for him, loved him, even. It was simply that he feared that feeling by itself might never be enough. Rita needed things. She didn't want a life of Waffle House hamburgers and fifty-cent tips, a life of clipping coupons and shopping at K mart. She didn't want trailer parks and used cars, soap operas and wasted afternoons. She wanted to make something of herself. And Connie wanted that for her too, only sometimes that frightened him. Sometimes thinking there might come a time when she wanted more than he could give her, thinking of her with the painter or someone else, sometimes thinking these things really frightened him.

A quiet noise came out of the valley — the scraping of feet on concrete. Connie froze. He listened, watched the trees at the top of the hill and the path leading down the center of the graveyard. It stopped. He eyed Mays, who was searching the darkness, his face hard. The scraping started again, and Connie cut back to the hill, listening. Two men walked out of the trees and the stones and into the clearing. They were walking slowly, one of them limping.

"Shit," Mays said. "What the shit is that?"

"Bums," Connie said. "There's a bunch of 'em down by the tracks. They got a regular camp."

The man with the limp took a harmonica out of his pocket and started blowing. It didn't sound like anything, only stray notes floating out across the valley. Connie thought of the old man again, of his friend who played the harmonica. This wouldn't be Kenny. Kenny was a kid with long blond hair, a ponytail. This man was clearly older, his hair cut short. Was the old man down there in his grave? Could he hear the music through the thicket? Connie pictured him laid out like a corpse in the pitch dark. He hoped the music wouldn't bring him out into the cemetery. He reached into his pocket and fingered the coin. Some lucky piece.

Mays picked up the flashlight, shielded the beam, and shined it onto his watch. He switched it off and laid it back at his feet. "They better get the fuck on outta there."

"Or what?" Connie said.

Mays looked at him hard, slightly surprised. "Or I'll beat the shit outta you, kid."

Connie watched a bead of sweat run down Mays's temple, the muscles flex in his jaw. He looked back down at the two men in the graveyard. They had stopped now about halfway down the hill, the one with the harp still blowing random notes, the other looking around through the graves. Bums. He played back the scene at the Waffle House, giving the old man the shirt and buying him the hamburgers. He remembered the jerk in the yellow golf shirt, how he'd swaggered over to the table, how he'd pointed at the old man. That's what you was in the ring, asshole. That's what you are now.

But it wasn't true. It wasn't true unless he made it come true. And he was determined not to do that. Rita would help him, but he needed to help her too. He needed something to give her. A big log house on a good piece of land, mountains and a river, a place to grow. Something solid, something more than the painter could give her. Nice clothes, nice cars, horses, cattle, sheep. All the things you could buy with a bag full of money.

The man with the harp sat down in the middle of the carriage path, said something to his friend, then banged the harp on the side of his leg and started playing again. This time the tune was slow and mournful, the notes bending into each other, bending into the frogs' croaking again from the gorge. The other man sat down beside him. He listened for a minute, swaying a little to his right, then he lay down in the path and folded his arms across his chest.

"What the fuck?" Mays said.

"They must be drunk."

Mays leaned over and picked up the flashlight. He shielded the beam and angled it on his wrist. "I'll give 'em ten minutes. Then they better be the fuck gone."

Connie liked seeing Mays bothered, liked watching him sweat. He wanted to say something to rub it in, but he knew better. He only sat there on the wall of the terrace in the deep shadow of the oak and watched the man with the mouth harp lie down beside his friend.

Mays dropped the flashlight into the grass and propped his elbows on his knees. There was the pistol again wedged under his belt. Connie caught himself staring at it — a blue large-framed revolver with black rubber grips, probably a .357 or a .44. In his memory, the cylinder and the barrel came down again over his eye. He reached up and fingered his eyebrow. It was sore and swollen, crusty with dried blood.

A bright light flared near the gate at the top of the hill, then shot a wide beam down the carriage path. The two men sat up in the road, shielding their eyes, then pushed to their feet. They staggered up the far hill and disappeared into the shadows and the stones. The light held for a minute, shooting a wide yellow tunnel down the center of the graveyard, then it eased a little farther down the hill and paused.

"Could be a cruiser," Mays said. "I don't like that. Ain't supposed to be no more cruisers coming through here till morning."

"Yeah, but that's good," Connie said. "If they suspected anything, they wouldn't be running a cruiser in here."

Mays nodded. "That's about the first bright thing I heard you say. You oughta use that brain more."

"Could be anything though," Connie said. "Could be just a couple of kids looking for a place to park."

"At this hour?"

"Why not?"

The headlights backed out of the cemetery and faded behind the stones and the trees screening the gate.

Mays stared for a second at the abandoned stretch of darkness. "Maybe."

"What else would it be?" Connie said.

"I don't know. And that's what I don't like about it."

They sat for several minutes, staring up at the top of the gate and the black wall of trees. Connie had a feeling the headlights would come back, but they didn't. "Kids," he said. "A cruiser would've come straight on down the road."

"Maybe."

"The bums scared 'em."

Mays tilted his head toward the hill behind them.

Something moved near the top, a crackling of brush. They turned and listened. It crackled again, but there were only the stones and the trees and the shadows. Mays slipped the pistol out of his belt and clutched it against his leg. Connie held his breath and listened.

Thirty yards up the hill the weight lifter stepped around a tree. He walked toward them slowly, watching where his feet came down in the shadows. Mays relaxed and wedged the pistol back under his belt. He turned around again to watch the valley, and Connie turned with him. The weight lifter eased up behind them and sat down on the other side of Mays.

"Well?" Mays watched the spot where the two bums had vanished into the gravestones.

"Nothing but them two tramps. There's a little fire way down there by the tracks. Two or three hundred yards down there, I guess. More tramps, most likely. It ain't no problem."

"That where they headed?"

"Most likely."

"They see you?"

"Nope."

"You see what that car was?"

"No. I just seen the lights."

"I don't like that," Mays said. "It was too much luck."

"Don't knock it," the weight lifter said. "It balances out. The tramps was bad luck." He stretched his legs out in front of him, and Connie saw for the first time a pistol on him too, a small revolver holstered around his right ankle. Connie stared down at the handle sticking out of his sock. That changed some things.

Mays picked up his flashlight again and checked his watch. "Thirteen minutes and that woman better come strolling on down that hill."

"Did Tommy say to call him tonight?" the weight lifter said.

"Tomorrow. We just wrap things up here and go on home. He'll call us in the morning."

"What about the money?"

"We'll count it somewhere and I'll take it home. Supposed to be two hundred."

The weight lifter smiled. "Maybe there'll be three and we can split one."

Mays dropped the flashlight between his feet. "Let's just hope there's two. I don't wanna have to explain nothing less."

Two hundred thousand dollars all in one lump. Connie wondered what it would be. Fifties, hundreds? Even that would be a hell of a bundle. Imagine all that in thousand-dollar stacks. How thick was a stack of twenty fifties? And two hundred of those? He didn't know, but it would be a hell of a bundle of money. And two hundred thousand was enough to buy a nice spread almost anywhere. Two hundred thousand dollars wasn't an empty promise. It was a real ticket west.

"He know what to do?" The weight lifter nodded toward Connie.

"He better," Mays said, giving Connie a glance. "He ain't gonna get another chance to learn."

The owl called again from across the river, twice, and the wind made a dry noise in the trees. A few frogs still belched by the creek, and the crickets sang with them. Then there was another kind of noise — a clicking of heels on concrete. They sat absolutely still and listened. It grew louder and clearer. A woman came out of the stones and trees at the top of the hill — a short, stocky woman in a dark business suit. She walked quickly, her eyes glued to the carriage path, a briefcase swinging heavy in her left hand. She disappeared for a second behind the brick wall of a terrace, then came out on the other side.

"Watch her close," Mays said.

The weight lifter answered, "I'm watching."

The woman walked halfway down the hill, then a little farther, turned to her left, and stepped ten yards into the gravestones. She dropped the briefcase behind a large gray tablet, turned, and stepped back onto the path. She walked up the hill the same way she'd walked down — quickly, with great determination, eyes stuck to the carriage path.

Mays put his hand on the weight lifter's shoulder. "She's supposed to be parked across the street in that empty station. Run up to the road and see if she gets in a car and leaves."

The weight lifter nodded. He got up, walked back up the hill and into the stones and trees.

"We'll just wait," Mays said.

Connie didn't say anything.

"We'll just sit here and be cool and wait."

"I can wait," Connie said.

"You keep your eyes on that headstone, kid. I don't want you to have no trouble finding it."

But Connie wouldn't have any trouble finding it. He knew that. In fact, he felt like something inside him was drawing him to it. A deep need operating like radar, homing in on the little terrace of graves, the gray tablet, and the briefcase lying on the ground behind it. No, finding it was not the part he'd have trouble with. Every ounce of his energy would take him to it.

"Don't move outta my sight, kid. Go straight down there, pick it up, and come straight back here."

"I think I can handle it," Connie said.

Mays leaned up and propped his elbows on his knees, and Connie caught himself staring again at the pistol. The handle and half of the trigger guard stuck out of his belt, but the pistol was wedged tight against his back. If he'd only lean down a little farther, Connie knew he could get a good grip. The thought of it now made his heart rush. If Mays would only lean down a little more, he could jerk the pistol right out of his belt.

Connie stared up toward the gravestone that marked the briefcase, then looked back at the revolver. Any minute, the weight lifter would come walking down the hill. He stared off toward the gorge where the frogs and the crickets were still making noise. Something felt wrong, uncomfortable. Then he knew what it was. His hands were shaking. He slipped them under his thighs. No, he didn't want to do that. He took a long breath and slid them out, let them rest on his knees. He glanced again at the black handle of the pistol. If Mays would only lean over a little farther, a foot farther, he could ease his left hand over and grab it. "What time is it?" he said.

Mays reached down to pick up the flashlight, his back bending away from the handle. Connie trembled. He lifted his left hand off his leg. It hovered over his knee, shaking.

Mays straightened up. "What the fuck you need the time for? It's time you did what I tell you to do."

Connie didn't say anything, only tried to steady himself. He slipped his hands back under his thighs and took a breath. Wind rustled in the trees, and he listened to the frogs and crickets by the creek and waited for his heart to calm. He heard the weight lifter trotting back down the hill, but he didn't turn around.

"Heads up," Mays said.

The weight lifter squatted beside Mays on the edge of the wall. He took a second to catch his breath. "She's gone. Walked right over to the filling station, got in a Volvo, and drove north up Riverside. Back over to the motel, I guess."

"That's good," Mays said. "She's a good mama. Gone to wait for her phone call."

"So let's get the money and get outta here."

Mays turned and shoved a finger into Connie's arm. "All right, kid, this is it. Don't do nothing dumb."

Connie stood up. He stared out across the valley of statues and stones to the hill beyond it, the little terrace beside the carriage path where the gray tablet hid the briefcase.

"Stay on the left one, kid. You hear me?"

Connie looked down into the valley. Mays meant the carriage paths up the hill. Three of them merged in the center of the valley and climbed the hill in different directions. The path on the right ran up toward the gate, but both the center path and the left would get him to the money. The shortest route was the center — it ran straight up the hill. But too much of it lay hidden by trees and monuments. The path to the left made a long circle toward the gorge and was twice the distance to the top. Mays liked it because it offered a clear view all the way.

"And don't fuck up."

Connie walked across the terrace, across the plot below it, and downhill toward the valley. He crossed the carriage path the old man had taken him down on the way to the open grave and climbed down three more terraces of graves. When he reached the spot where the three concrete paths converged, he wanted to turn around and see if Mays and the weight lifter were still on the wall in the darkness of the oak, but he didn't. He just took the left path and followed it across the valley.

All around him flat-slabbed graves lay scattered in the dark grass, and on his right, tall brick- and marble-walled terraces climbed the long hill. He walked quickly, wanting to turn around and check the darkness and the trees, but he knew not to. He looked straight up the path and kept on walking.

Fifty yards down the valley the path cut sharply to the right and started climbing the hill. Connie turned with it, the terraces of graves rising now on his right and his left. He passed a marble woman on a large pedestal, behind her a curtain of dark ivy draped over a wall, and an odd feeling passed through him, as though she had gestured to him somehow with her eyes, a sign of understanding or recognition. The graveyard beyond blossomed with hundreds of stones and crosses fading into the trees shading the center of the hill.

Another path branched off into the gravestones to his left — tablets and crosses falling away toward the river, six or seven large obelisks, and an angel with one wing — but he passed on by it, kept walking straight up the hill. He was thinking of the eyes behind him, not only the marble eyes of the woman but the eyes of Mays and the weight lifter somewhere among the stones and trees of the ridge. He was thinking of the pistol wedged under Mays's belt, the pistol in the holster strapped to the weight lifter's ankle. But those pistols weren't the real threat. He knew that. So did Mays and the weight lifter. The real threat was the pistol that Pinyon was holding on Carl and the kid.

Seventy more yards and he was almost at the crest of the hill. He stopped beside a huge obelisk on his left. In faint letters, the stone said LAMAR. He climbed up on the wall of the plot and scouted the graveyard sloping toward the river.

Over the wall of a stone terrace Connie could see the top of the gray tablet where the woman had dropped the briefcase. He felt his heart rush. Two hundred thousand dollars, and he was forty yards from it. He brushed the sweat from his neck and looked behind him into the valley. The trees where he'd left Mays and the weight lifter were a solid three hundred yards away, and in the shadows he couldn't even see the gray obelisk below them. Maybe the two men were still there. Or maybe they weren't. By now they could be just about anywhere on the side of the hill. He turned toward the tablet where the money lay and thought of Rita, of the five gold rings in her ear. Two hundred thousand would buy a nice place almost anywhere. Two hundred thousand would make a real start, more than a start. You could get lost with that kind of money. And in a place like Montana you could really get lost.

He balled his right hand into a fist and pressed it against his chest. His heart was beating fast now, the way it beat sometimes before a fight. The wind stirred the stench from the paper mill, but he took a deep breath anyway and stepped off the wall.

When he rounded the corner of the next terrace, he saw the briefcase. It was leaning at the foot of a large granite stone. He walked over to it. The face of the stone said WOOD-MEN OF THE WORLD MEMORIAL and, under that, HENRY LAFAY-ETTE GATES. A wave of fear rushed through him. He felt light-headed. He glanced back across the valley toward the giant oak on the hill. The men were over there somewhere, but he couldn't see them. They were over there in the trees and they had pistols, but they were a good three hundred and fifty yards away. Or had they followed him down the hill? He checked out the graveyard to his right, where the graves and the trees fell off toward the railroad tracks and the river. Beyond the pines across the river he could hear the cars on the interstate. He turned around and looked across the hill behind him. Stones stood all along the crest — a huge angel with broken arms, and behind it a giant cross with an angel under it. A wave of fear swept through him again. He knew if he ran past those angels and down that hill, he could follow the tracks to the highway. A mile or so down those tracks and he'd be at the edge of town. Across the valley lay three hundred and fifty yards of darkness, and even if they'd followed him to the foot of the hill, they'd never catch him. The poolhall was open all night. If he could get down there, he could borrow a car, pick up Rita, and be gone for good. Jeff Willett might be down there, or Charley Goins or Bud Fowler. They'd help him out. But the pistol on Carl was the real threat. Tommy and his boys knew that. The pistol on Carl and the kid was what they were counting on. He took a breath. Three hundred and fifty yards of darkness. Maybe a little less. If he grabbed the briefcase and ran, they'd never catch him.

He bent down and picked it up. It was heavy, solid with money, and the feel of it made him shiver. He hadn't expected it to be so heavy, so solid. He ran his fingers over the knobby side, gripped the handle tight, turned and checked the hill behind him. The two angels kept a quiet watch over the graves. Fear rushed hard and made him shake. He stood still for a second, holding the briefcase, letting his heart calm. The fear struck again, but he fought it and ran.

Connie crossed the carriage path on the crest of the hill, ran past the angel with broken arms and across two terraces of graves. The cemetery opened up into another long hill of stones, and the fire of the hobos burned small as a match flame at the far end of it. To his left rose the giant cross and the angel beneath it, then a sharp drop and a wall of trees in front of the railroad tracks. He turned toward the tracks and saw a man run out of those trees. He stopped. Another man came around the corner of a high brick terrace thirty yards to his right. It was Pinyon.

Shit, Pinyon wasn't supposed to be here. Connie turned and ran hard back up the hill.

"Goddamnit," somebody said. "Get around that way. Get around there and cut him off."

Connie ran past the angel with no arms and back across the carriage path, then something caught his foot. He fell head-first into the grass, and the briefcase jumped out of his arms, slid five or six feet in front of him. He scrambled to his knees and picked it up. On his left stood the brick wall of a grave plot. He pushed himself up, climbed over it, and crouched. Two of the graves were aboveground — brick vaults with thick iron tops — and close together, not quite three feet apart. He crawled over, slid the briefcase between them, and wedged himself in on top of it.

He held his breath and listened. Footsteps ran across the carriage path and stopped. More footsteps came up the path, walking.

"Where'd he go to?" somebody said.

"He's around here," Pinyon said.

Connie took a slow breath. He was hot and light-headed, his fear pushing him almost to a panic. He tried to breathe easy, to calm himself and clear his head. The cool dew seeped into his jeans, and he wiped his eyes and thought about a soak in Rita's tub. A long cool soak.

Brush crackled out of the heart of the valley, then footsteps ran up a path to his left. He listened to them grow louder, all the way to the top of the hill. They stopped somewhere above him and walked, heels dragging, down the carriage path behind him.

"What the fuck?" Mays said, winded, breathing heavily.

"He ran back this way," Pinyon said. "You see him?"

A flashlight beam cut through the grass in front of Connie's face. It slid off toward the wall, halfway up it, then over.

"The shitass. Can you believe that crazy shitass?" Mays was still huffing, out of breath.

"He's around in here somewhere," the weight lifter said. "We would've seen him if he'd run on down the hill."

"All right," Pinyon said. "Let's scatter. Put a circle around this place, and let's make sure he stays in it."

Connie listened to the footsteps move up and down the carriage path. He tried to picture where they were, where they were going. If he could get behind them, he could work his way down to the railroad tracks and into town. The footsteps grew fainter on the path, fading in both directions. He lay still and waited.

"Listen, Holtzclaw, you might as well come on out. Just give us the money and we'll send you on home." Pinyon's voice was quiet, calm. He was somewhere in front of Connie and moving down the hill.

Connie lay quiet, face down between the two vaults, the briefcase still under his chest. He listened hard for footsteps, for movement. Across the river the cars still roared on the interstate, and out of the gorge the frogs opened up again in long, deep belches. But no footsteps.

"This is stupid, man. You ain't gonna get outta here." From the sound of his voice, Pinyon was thirty or forty yards down the hill now and moving toward the valley. "Come on, man. It's too hot for this shit. We could all be home right now drinking a beer."

That sounded good, real good. To be home in his own air-conditioned trailer, lying on his bed and drinking a cool Pabst. Or better still, to be soaking in Rita's tub, to be soaking in her tub with a beer in his hand. Then a strange thought came to Connie, a thought that carried a disturbing sense of finality. It occurred to him that he might never do those things again. Not in that trailer, not in that apartment. No, he probably never would do those things again. He had broken with this town now, and there was no going back. But wasn't that okay? Wasn't that what he was really after?

He waited a few seconds, then he crawled forward to the edge of the wall. He eased his head over the top. Pinyon was fifty or sixty yards down the hill, walking toward the valley, his flashlight throwing a yellow beam around the stones. Connie checked the graveyard to his right and left. Only the darkness and the trees and the stones.

He reached back between the brick vaults and grabbed the briefcase, then inched across the grave plot to the wall facing the carriage path, crawled through the gate, and crouched. The carriage path was empty, but across the path a beam of light shot onto the angel with no arms. Connie crouched lower against the wall. He wouldn't be able to get over the hill. It was too risky. But maybe he could work back into the stones and follow the path to the edge of the cemetery and the tracks. He crawled to the lower edge of the terrace wall and looked around it. There was plenty of cover in the graveyard. If he was quiet and careful, he might just work his way down to those tracks. But they were on two sides of him now. No, all around him. They had him in a circle. He'd have to remember that.

"Listen," Pinyon said. "This is already getting old. Just throw out the money and we'll all go home." His voice was much fainter now, moving farther into the valley.

Connie gripped the briefcase tight and slid around the corner of the wall. He hurried a few quick steps into the next plot and lay flat on the ground behind a marble tablet. He listened. Only the cars on the interstate, the frogs, and the wind coming up from the river. He eased his head around the gravestone and looked across the carriage path. The beam of light was gone. He checked out the valley. Pinyon's flashlight was a yellow cane tapping toward the bottom of the hill.

He pushed himself onto his hands and knees and crept toward the next terrace. Eighty yards in front of him the wind rustled in a thick cluster of trees. That was the place he wanted to get to, the dark silhouette at the foot of the valley. From those trees he'd have good cover down to the tracks. He stopped behind the stone wall of the grave plot. A diesel roared in the distance, a shifting of gears. He held still and waited, the briefcase wedged under his chest.

"Asshole," a voice said. It was behind him, up the hill some and off to his left.

He turned and looked over his shoulder. A beam of light came around the big LAMAR obelisk, zigzagging toward him between the graves. He pushed himself close against the wall. No, this wouldn't work. He needed to get around the corner of the wall. He pushed the briefcase out in front of him and snaked behind it.

"Asshole," the voice said again.

Connie stopped. It was a voice he didn't recognize. Maybe it belonged to Fry, the man Tommy was looking for. But then, who was back at the fish camp watching Carl and the kid? Tommy, he thought. Sure, Tommy could do it by himself because he knew Carl wouldn't give him any trouble. Tommy could do it by himself because he knew the truth about Carl. He's seen him in action. He knew Carl was a coward.

He pushed the briefcase out in front of him and started to crawl again, quietly, slowly, only a few feet at a time. When he rounded the corner, he turned around to face the valley and lay down on his stomach, close against the terrace wall.

Footsteps drew near, a quiet but clear scuffing on stone. The man was walking along the top of the wall. The footsteps stopped, and the beam of light shot through the grass ten yards in front of Connie's face. He squeezed the handle of the briefcase, got ready to run. The light moved down the hill and into a cluster of small stones, then came back and stopped five feet from the corner of the terrace.

Connie smelled something odd, a sharp earthy smell. The light moved down the hill again to a terrace of large obelisks. It climbed up the side of one, came back down, and climbed another. The smell again, earthy and metallic. Something was crawling on his left hand. He lifted it off the ground and looked down. It was black with ants. He held his breath and rubbed the hand in the grass, hard and slow, trying not to make noise. The hand caught fire, and the fire moved up to his wrist. He rubbed it harder in the grass, trying to put it out, trying not to make noise, trying not to panic.

The footsteps moved away from him on the wall, and he crawled backward three or four feet, dragging his hand hard through the grass. When he thought he'd brushed it clean, he pushed himself to his knees. His heart was pounding again, the pain still eating into the back of his fingers and hand. He shook the hand and balled it into a loose fist. He could already feel it swelling around the knuckles the way it swelled after a long fight.

He sat back on his heels and raised his head over the top of the wall. The man was standing on the far corner of the terrace, his back toward Connie, the flashlight shining into the valley. Connie eased back down and slowly balled his hand tighter. The pain flared around his knuckles, moved down the back of his hand. As long as Fry was standing on the wall, he was stuck. And if Fry, or whoever he was, decided to walk ten yards toward the river, he'd see him for sure.

Connie felt in the grass for a rock. Only a few leaves and twigs. He backed up a few more feet and felt around the base of the wall. A few pebbles about the size of marbles. He sat up on his knees and tossed one into the valley. He crouched and waited. Nothing. Not much of a trick, he knew that, something straight from a bad Western. But he couldn't think of anything else. He sat back up and tossed another pebble, farther this time. It made a slight crack against a stone.

The man didn't move from the wall. Connie listened. Only the traffic on the interstate, the frogs in the gorge. A dog barked somewhere in the distance behind him, then another. No wind now, or footsteps. Then he saw the beam of light slide past the corner ten yards in front of him. It turned and cut into the valley, and the man walked past the corner of the terrace and followed it down the hill.

Connie waited until he faded among the tall stones halfway down, then he slid the briefcase out in front of him and crawled into the next plot. He listened. The man's footsteps moved through the valley, drifting steadily away. Connie crept toward the dark silhouette of trees, five and ten yards at a time.

When he reached their deep shadow, he pushed five yards into it, stood up behind the trunk of a large oak, and looked around. Two flashlight beams, about fifty yards apart, were crisscrossing down the valley, moving toward the far ridge where he had waited with Mays and the weight lifter. He clamped down on the briefcase and moved toward the foot of the hill.

Quicker now, in a half crouch, he watched his steps closely. Thirty yards through the trees the hill dropped off in a steep grassy bank to the tracks. At the foot of that bank Connie saw another light. The beam cut straight up the slope and onto his face.

"There he is!" Mays yelled. "There he is!"

Connie bolted hard to his left, back through the trees toward the valley. The lights in the valley above him held for a second, then flashed down into the cluster of trees. He hugged the briefcase tight under his arms, brush and low branches slapping him on the shoulders and face. He raised a forearm and ran harder, dodging through the trees.

"Come on!" Mays shouted. "He's down here!"

Maybe he could cut down the hill and try to cross the tracks? No, they had pistols and they just might use them. He ran hard. The gorge was a hundred and fifty yards in front of him. And inside the thicket lay the old man's grave. They'd never find him there. But if they saw him run into that thicket, there was no way out, that's just where he'd stay.

He ran on, branches slapping past his outstretched arm, then the trees opened suddenly at the edge of a twenty-foot bank. He stopped for a second and looked down at the gorge — to his right the creek flowing toward the river, to his left the edge of the thicket. He could hear Mays tearing through the brush behind him. Could he still cut down the hill to the tracks? The brush crackled. He sat on the bank, slid down, and ducked into the dark edge of the thicket.

A flashlight beam came over the side of the gorge. It went to the thicket and ran up and down the edge. Connie watched Mays drop to the bank and start his slide. He turned and crawled into the pitch dark, slowly but steadily, trying to be quiet, trying without luck to control his fear. If Mays came in now with the flashlight, he'd never make it to the old man's grave.

11

"WHO'S OUT there?" the old man said.

"Sssh," Connie said. "It's me, the guy that gave you the shirt. Turn that lantern down."

"What for?"

"Turn it down, goddamnit."

The light behind the leaves dimmed to a murky green stain floating in the black of the thicket.

"What you doing?" the old man said.

"Sssh. Be quiet."

The old bum pushed back the thick magnolia branches covering the mouth of the grave. "Come on in here."

Connie shoved the briefcase through the opening, lifted his leg carefully over the jagged bars, and crawled into the hill. The lantern burned dull in the middle of the room. The metal box and the paper bags sat against the wall behind it, and the sleeping bag lay in the middle of the floor, stretched out across the mattress of ratty newspaper. The old man crawled over to it and sat down.

Connie sat on the briefcase. "Is that the only light you got?"

"I got some candles. I got a flashlight."

"How 'bout we just light a couple of those candles and turn that lantern off?"

The bum gave him a curious look. "You want candles? We

can light some candles. All the same to me." He turned around and picked up one of the paper bags. He took out two candles and a box of wooden matches, lit the candles, and stood them up in empty sardine tins. He leaned up and turned out the lantern.

The grave fell very dark, only two small points of light. The closeness made Connie gasp — the same smothering darkness he felt as a child when Carl would lock him in the closet. He remembered the panic of the door closing, the jerking and shoving at the knob, the way the fear grew into nausea.

Connie watched the candles struggling to make a steady flame, their faint light bleeding into each other. One of them rose up off the ground and floated across the darkness. The old man's eyes, the shadows of his wrinkles, his yellow beard, moved behind it at the edge of the light. The flame came down against the far wall, steadied, and sat still.

"Somebody after you?" the old man whispered.

"Something like that."

"How come?"

"I got into a little trouble. Nothing to worry about. Maybe I can just wait here till they leave."

"Police?"

"No, just some guys."

"They out there in the graveyard?"

"Yeah."

"Looking for you?"

Connie balled his left hand into a fist and felt the pain again around his knuckles. "That's right."

"How come?"

"A little misunderstanding, that's all. It'll be all right. Maybe I can just wait here for a little while?"

"They won't never find you in here," the old man said. "They wouldn't find you in here in a thousand years."

He hoped that was true. But he didn't want to be here for a thousand years either. He remembered the smell of mothballs and musty wool, the close air going thick and stale. He remembered the sticky plastic laundry bags, the sharp heels of his mother's shoes turned upside down on the floor. "Maybe not," he said. "But they won't give up easy."

"They won't never find you in here."

"Maybe."

"Never," the old man said. "It ain't possible."

Parts of the room began to lighten slightly as Connie's eyes adjusted to the dark. The old man was sitting on the sleeping bag, his legs crossed under him, Indian style. He placed his left hand on his knee, and Connie read again in the edge of the candlelight the word tattooed across his fingers. There was only one place you got a tattoo like that. It was home-made, scratched with a straight pin or a needle or a staple. Prison. Connie wondered what the old man had done and how long he'd been in for doing it. He studied that hand — the crooked lines of the H, the crossed line in the T almost faded away. Then he studied the rest of the man. The candlelight barely reaching him from opposite directions made the bum an eerie picture — the sides of his head and beard glowed deep orange while his face and eyes glimmered faintly in the dark.

"What you got in that suitcase?" the old man said.

"Some of my brother's stuff. Some of his business stuff."

"It ain't nothing you stole, is it?"

Connie peered hard into the darkness between the two candles. "No. Just some business papers. My brother's a lawyer. These are important papers, evidence. They could get some big people in trouble."

"It ain't nothing to me if you stole it." The old man rubbed the backs of his hands, then cracked his knuckles. "People steal things all the time. It ain't good, but they do it. One man ain't gonna turn nothing around."

Connie stared into the darkness that was the old bum's face. "No, these are just some papers, my brother's papers.

They ain't worth nothing to nobody else. He's a lawyer in town here."

"He the one that give me the shirt?"

"That's right."

The old man rocked back and forth between the borders of light. He fought back a small cough and cleared his throat quietly. "That suitcase how come them guys chasing you?"

"That's right."

"I been chased a lot," the old man said. "Mostly I been chased off, not chased after. Off trains, outta hotels, bars, eating joints. I even been chased off sidewalks. A man gets tired of getting chased off all the time. It ain't right, people always trying to chase you off." He leaned up and studied Connie's face, then sat back in the darkness between the two candles. "Somebody beat you up, huh?"

"That's about the size of it."

"That ain't no fun neither. I think I'd go ahead and give 'em them papers. I don't like fights."

"I can't do that. It ain't that simple."

The old man rubbed the palms of his hands. "Sounds simple enough."

"Well, my brother might not think so. He'd lose his case, and these guys would get off."

"He'd lose a lotta money, huh?"

Connie watched the old bum's eyes move back and forth between the borders of light. "I don't know. I guess he might. And these guys would get off, that's what's important. He wouldn't like that."

"I lost a lotta money one time," the old man said.

"How was that?"

"They told me, but I forgot exactly. I think it had something to do with books."

"What kinda books?"

"I don't know?"

"You don't remember much, do you?"

"I got something that makes me that way. I had it a long time. They told me one time what it was."

"Who did?" Connie said.

"Folks that know that stuff."

Connie nodded. He stared for a minute into the darkness between the two candles. "Maybe that's good," he said. "If you can't remember nothing, you can't miss nothing. I don't know, but maybe if you can't miss nothing, you don't even want nothing."

"I miss things," the old man said.

"What's that?"

"Oh, I don't know. Lots of stuff." The old bum rubbed his hands and thought for a minute. "Tenderness," he said. "I miss tenderness. And comfort. Kenny, he missed that too. He talked a lot about that, he did."

Connie didn't say anything. The darkness and the panic had closed in on him again. It wasn't just the words. It was hearing the old man say them. They just weren't the kind of words anyone would ever expect him to say. Not a crazy old man who lived in a hole. But it was more than that. It was hearing him say them in this place — the one place where you lost everything, the place you were never supposed to leave.

"I ain't just talking about sleeping in a king-size bed in a big hotel room. I had some of that and other things too. That ain't it, that ain't it at all. You take Kenny. He had a tenderness about him. He cared a lot about folks, how they felt, what they thought. He'd sit up all night with you, Kenny would. He cared about things. That's all comfort is, a tenderness. He said that, Kenny did. You can have a tenderness around and live real fine just about anywhere."

"Maybe so," Connie said. Then Rita's presence seemed to pass through the grave — the touch of her hands and lips in the dark, the gentleness of her voice whispering across it. And suddenly he remembered the morning he'd first tried to tell her how much he cared for her, a morning after a bad loss, a TKO. He'd had his mouthpiece knocked out and had bitten clear through his tongue — three stitches. It was so swollen he could hardly talk, but he'd tried and he'd meant what he said, and what came out with those garbled words truly surprised him — something he never wanted to lose. Tenderness, he guessed, was as good a word for it as any.

The weight of Rita's body settled on him again, the easy wave she made of them in the dark, and then he recalled the argument they'd had that morning. He was sorry for that, sorry things had to be that way. "Hey," he said, "you know what tomorrow is?"

"Morning."

"Easter," Connie said. "Tomorrow's Easter."

"That's when Jesus was born."

"Christmas," Connie said. "That's Christmas. Easter's when he rose from the dead."

The old man nodded. "Yeah, I guess I knew that. He was born once, then he got born again."

Connie watched him leaning back into the dark.

"That'd be nice, wouldn't it?" the old man said.

"What's that?"

"To get up outta the grave like Jesus."

"Yeah, I guess that'd be nice, all right. Except you'd have to die first. But I don't know if he really did it. Makes a good story though."

"Everybody says he done it."

"Who's everybody?"

"She said he done it," the old man said. "That woman I told you about, she talked about it all the time. It was in all the songs that he done it."

"The woman that sang about the rivers?"

"That's right. And it was in all the songs that way."

"That's because it's a good story," Connie said. "People like to hear a good story."

The old man rocked in and out of the light, staring across the darkness at Connie. "Sure, I reckon they do," he said. "But I think he done it too. 'Cause if he didn't do it, then all the songs'd be wrong. And she didn't sing 'em that way, like they was wrong, I mean. You'd know it if you'd ever heard her sing 'em. I heard her lots of times. I heard —"

"Hey, is that a spider over there?" Connie shuddered.

The old man swung toward his left. "Where?"

"Right there behind that candle. I thought I saw something crawl under that bag."

The old bum hardly looked around. "Ain't no spiders in here. I already told you that."

"Well, maybe you ain't —"

Something rustled deep in the thicket. Connie's heart jumped. He turned toward the mouth of the grave and listened. It rustled again, a shuffling of leaves, then a branch snapped and Connie leaned over to his left and blew out one candle. The old man blew out the other one, and the grave went pitch black.

The darkness threw a chill into Connie that raised the hair on his arms and sent a quiver into his groin. This was all the bad darkness of the past, the suffocating dark of his mother's closet, Carl's laugh coming through the door, then fading off for hours. This was that darkness and many others, and with them the hot concrete dark of the county jail, the constant stench of urine, the sick fear. It started to come back to him now, that sick panic, but he fought it with another darkness, a good darkness, the kind he and Rita crawled into together. He thought of the way it closed out the rest of the world so that there was only the two of them, together and totally alone. That was a darkness he liked a lot, and they'd have a lot of that in Montana, the good darkness that closed out everything else. And every good darkness would break into a good light, into open land running to clear rivers and big mountains, into wide sky.

The rustling in the thicket grew louder. Then it stopped. "Goddamn this shit," somebody said. The voice was distant but clear.

"Go on," Mays said.

"Goddamn this shit."

"Go on."

And it started again — a snapping of brush, the heavy shuffling of leaves slowly growing louder. Every second it grew a little more distinct, a steady crackling moving closer. Connie could picture them out there on their hands and knees, the pistols wedged under their belts, the flashlights boring yellow beams into the thicket.

Then it got much louder. Connie held his breath and looked toward the mouth of the grave. There was only a solid pitch-black wall. Then a small circle of green light swept across a patch of it. Then it crossed again, a little higher.

"Goddamn this shit to hell," somebody said again.

They were very close, maybe only a few yards away. Connie's heart raced. He listened to the noise stalk toward him through the thicket. The ball of green light climbed onto the darkness and hung there, and he could see again the tiny veins in the magnolia leaves covering the mouth of the grave. A slight nausea turned in his stomach.

"You see something?" Mays said.

"Leaves."

The light moved off to Connie's left and disappeared, and the rustling started again. He heard the black leaves shake in the open mouth of the grave. His heart rushed, and the sickness wallowed in his stomach. The leaves shook a few seconds more, then settled, and the noise started moving off to his left and away. He listened to it fade, took a breath, and tried to steady himself.

Now he could hear the old man breathing across the grave, a long slow wheeze, and something about the steadiness of it, the calm, made him feel better. The two men crawled farther away toward the edge of the thicket, and after a few minutes their noise stopped entirely.

"Gone," the old man whispered.

"No way," Connie said. "They're still out there somewhere. They ain't giving up yet."

"One time I hid out all night under a tarp in this boxcar. Couldn't take a piss, couldn't hardly move. Afraid this Mexican was gonna cut my throat."

Connie didn't say anything.

"That was out West. I remember that real good."

Connie weighed a break for the highway. If he could just get to a car, everything would be fine. If he could get to Rita's house, they'd be a couple of hundred miles away by daylight. No, Tommy could be watching her place. That might be where they spotted him yesterday. He'd do better to get to a car and phone Rita, have her meet him somewhere. And what about Carl and the kid? He tried not to think about them. With Fry down here, Tommy must be getting impatient at the lodge.

"How 'bout lighting that candle?" he said.

But what about Carl and the kid?

Something scraped, and a light came on in the old man's hand. It swept to the floor, touched the candle, and caught.

Okay, if he could find a way to get Carl half the money, maybe that would satisfy Tommy. A hundred thousand dollars was a lot, and there wasn't any profit in hurting anybody. Tommy knew that. After all, wasn't Carl always saying how Tommy was just a businessman? And with his half Connie could still make a good start with Rita. It was still twice as much as he'd expected, twice what Carl had told him he'd get.

He felt a little faint. The dark was stuffy, he didn't seem to be able to get enough air. He watched the candle steady and took a breath through his mouth, then another. Rita and the good dark, the good touch, the tenderness he'd never really thought of as tenderness. Then he thought of the light the good dark led to, the sun on the fine blond hairs of Rita's arms, the sun on the five gold rings in her ear. And with that the painter, and the sickness came to him again.

A hundred thousand dollars was a good start, but two hundred would be twice the start. Two hundred thousand would buy them twice as much land, twice as many trees, twice as much sky. They could get lost for twice as long on two hundred thousand. He reached down and touched the briefcase under him. He hated the thought of giving up any of the money. But what would he do about Carl and the kid?

The old man slid forward on the sleeping bag and lay back in the darkness. "I got to stretch out here a little bit," he said. "It's my back. I got the bad joints."

Connie nodded.

So what about Carl? Carl was his brother, sure, and Carl had done a lot for him, but hadn't he also tried to cheat him? Hadn't Carl told him it was going to be a hundred and he was getting half? And all along it was going to be two hundred, and Carl was only planning to give him fifty. Sure, Carl was his brother, all right, but weren't things mostly like Rita said? And now, when it mattered most, here was Carl still trying to pull his shit.

Connie saw Carl again on the floor of the lodge. If he kept this money, he knew what might happen to him. He knew what might happen to the kid. Tommy Wilson might really make them pay. The nausea turned in his stomach. He didn't want to think about them. He didn't want to think he was responsible. And maybe he wasn't responsible for Carl. Carl had gotten himself into this mess. But Connie knew something else too. He *was* responsible for the boy. Only partly at first, but completely now because everybody's future was right in this briefcase. He thought about the kid lying naked on the mattress, chained to the radiator. He thought about his bruised eyes and swollen mouth. He was sorry he'd hit him, he really was. Hitting him was an awful thing to do. And suddenly Connie had an urge to apologize, to tell him how much he regretted it, that he'd had to do it to make him see they meant business.

But it was too late for that, and he knew it. Still, he was sorry all the same, and he hoped that Tommy had given his clothes back to him. He didn't like to think of him lying there naked. He didn't like to think of Tommy looking at him. The sickness hit harder, and Connie felt faint again. He knew only one thing for sure. He wasn't going to give up the money. The money meant a new life — a new life for him, a new life for Rita — and he wasn't about to give that up.

He listened to the old man breathing, a deep even wheeze that broke occasionally into a snore. No, he wasn't giving up the money. The man in the yellow golf shirt was wrong. That's what you were in the ring, that's what you are now. It wasn't true, and he was going to make sure it never was true. Rita would help him and he'd help her. They'd make sure they had something good, they'd make sure they had each other. Rita's leaving town wasn't really a problem. He knew that. A job at the Waffle House wouldn't be hard to drop. And whatever promises the painter had made her were no match for two hundred thousand dollars.

Connie looked at the old man lying on his back on the sleeping bag. He sat up, dragged out the briefcase, and laid it across his lap. He popped the clasps easy and opened it. It was full of money, thick stacks of bills tied together with rubber bands, and the look of it sent another shiver through him. He slid ten or twelve bills out of one of the stacks and held them up to the candlelight. They were hundreds. He closed the briefcase quietly, crawled over, and slipped the bills under the base of the lantern.

But what about Carl and the kid? Carl with his face bashed in, the boy naked and chained to the radiator?

The sickness struck Connie hard again, and this time he

knew he was going to vomit. He leaned down, opened his mouth, and took a deep breath. It didn't help. He took another, and tried to think of Rita and the place they'd have in Montana. He felt weak, he was going to vomit. He turned and crawled to the mouth of the grave. He eased over the bars, crawled through the branches of the magnolia and ten yards into the black of the thicket.

The nausea wallowed deep in his chest. He waited for a minute, on his hands and knees, trying to breathe. Then it came on hard, cut off his air entirely, and he retched. His eyes watered and his breath came back for a second. Then he retched again, trying not to make noise, but he was making noise, and he knew it. He leaned over a little farther and vomited.

When it was over he felt winded and weak, but better. Then it came hard again, vomit spewing from his throat and nose. He wiped his face on his hand and rubbed the hand on the ground. The wind made a small rustle in the trees above him, and a dog yelped far off toward town. He sat for a minute, resting and catching his breath. Then he pulled up his shirttail, wiped his mouth again, and crawled back into the grave.

Connie sat back down on the briefcase and stretched his legs out in front of him. He felt better. Weak, but better. He had to decide what to do about Carl and the kid. There was one thing he could do. He'd known all along but hadn't wanted to face it. It wasn't a good choice, but if he couldn't think of anything else, he could always call the police. He could get out of this hole, get to a phone, and call the police. He hated the thought of it. He hated the thought of Carl in jail, but Carl had gotten himself into this mess. No, Carl had gotten them both into it, and he knew the chance he was taking. He hated the thought of Carl in prison, but what if things were turned around? What would Carl do? Hadn't Carl already tried to cheat him? No, forget that. He wasn't like Carl.

But calling the police might be the only answer. It might be the only thing he could do to make sure no one got hurt.

But doing that would mean the police would be after him too. Yes, if he called the police, they'd come right after him. Maybe that's just the way it had to be. Then again, he could wait a few hours before he phoned. He could wait a few hours, and he and Rita could put some miles behind them. That was only fair. A few hundred miles was fair enough. Of course, by then, Carl and the kid might be dead. No, probably not. Tommy was a businessman. He just wanted his money. He didn't need any dead bodies lying around. Besides, a few hundred miles was only fair.

The old man snored soundly. Connie stepped toward the candlelight and picked up the two paper bags sitting near the wall. In the first bag he found a Walkman and six or seven tapes. He sat it down, opened the other one, and found five candles, a box of matches, and a flashlight. Kenny's flashlight, the old man had said. He flipped the switch and threw a quick circle of light onto the wall.

He wedged the flashlight into his back pocket and stepped over to the mouth of the grave. Holding down the magnolia branches, he could hear the wind in the very top of the thicket, the gentle movement of leaves. They were out there somewhere — maybe just beyond the thicket, maybe in some other part of the graveyard. They were out there somewhere looking for him. They wouldn't give it up that easily. But he had to move. He had to get to a car and pick up Rita, put some miles behind them so he could call the police.

"Hey, old man?" he whispered.

The bum didn't answer, his breathing still deep and even.

"Hey," Connie said again.

The old man didn't stir.

If they were out there at the edge of the gorge, he'd have to wait. But if they were in some other part of the graveyard, he might be able to get down to the tracks. Where would they be looking if they thought he'd climbed out of the thicket? He listened, he thought about the probabilities. Were they still watching the gorge? Come on. He could wait and listen all night, but the only way to be sure was to go out there and take a look.

He glanced back at the dim candle burning in the back of the grave, the paper bags, the old man lying half in the light and half in the darkness. He reached back and picked up the briefcase. The only thing to do now was to see for himself. He stepped back to the mouth of the grave, lifted the briefcase over the bars, and climbed out into the pitch black. He sat for a second outside the magnolia branches. The wind moved in the leaves above him. If they weren't waiting outside the thicket, it would be all right, the tracks were only a hundred yards or so away. He could move along the side of the gorge, slide down the bank above the tracks, and use the bank for cover.

He pushed the briefcase in front of him and crawled after it, going very slowly, trying to be absolutely quiet. But every step made a noise in the brush, so he moved only a few feet at a time. When he reached the edge of the thicket, he stopped a foot or two inside the cover.

The frogs belched along the creek, a wind blew across the gorge. He pulled back the branches and looked out. Only the creek moving down the gorge toward the river, the brick faces of the crypts dug into the side of the far bank. He cut to the top of that bank. Nothing. Then to the top of the left bank. Only the trees and the monuments on the point.

Connie let the brush close and eased back into the thicket. Okay, maybe he could move along the right side of the gorge, cross the creek, and work his way to the tracks. Then he could get to town and a phone. Sure, it was only a mile or so if it was that far.

He pulled back the brush again and peered out. A beam of light flashed down the hill and across the creek. He let the brush close easy and sat very still. His hands were shaking. He folded his arms and tried to stay loose. Okay, he knew where they were, one of them anyway, and that was something.

The light jumped back to the top of the bank, and a gray figure walked out to the edge of the gorge and shined the beam down over the thicket. Connie ducked back a little farther. The man's face was too dark, but his head and shoulders had the shape of the weight lifter. Odds were good that the others were off in different parts of the graveyard. Maybe they figured he'd climbed up one of the back walls. Maybe they'd posted the weight lifter at the mouth of the gorge in case they were wrong.

The beam of light played around the creek and across it. Connie listened for voices or footsteps, but there were only the frogs by the creek and off in the distance the cars on the interstate. Then a faint rumble far off to his right. It was odd and a little frightening, something like a distant earthquake crawling closer. It picked up and came on steadily. Then he knew what it was and a sharp excitement went through him. He felt in his pocket for his car keys. He squeezed them tight and listened to the dull, steady thunder, lumbering and heavy. It was very close now, right in front of him, rolling by and roaring at him from both sides. Yard speed, he remembered the old man saying. Yard speed, where the bums swung on and off. If he could get by the weight lifter and get on one of those boxcars, he could be at his car in fifteen minutes. Twenty or thirty minutes later, he and Rita could be gone.

The train came on strong, a noise on both sides. Connie's heart pounded in his chest. He had to do something now, it wouldn't go on much longer. The beam of the flashlight turned toward the thicket, and he pulled back into the heavy brush. It passed right by him and moved to the foot of the far bank. The train came on as the flashlight climbed up and down the bank, moving toward the mouth of the gorge. Connie squeezed the handle of the briefcase. The beam of light ran toward the tracks, turned back toward the cluster of trees, and disappeared. He looked along the top of the bank. The weight lifter was gone. He clutched the briefcase. He ran out of the brush.

The train still came strong, a roar on both sides, and he ran hard toward it, the briefcase tucked like a football under his arm, his right hand still locked around the handle. He jumped the creek and ran past the brick crypts in the side of the hill. The train's rumble was becoming unbalanced now, the heavier roar moving off to his left, off to the north.

He ran hard toward the edge of the bank.

"There he is, goddamnit!"

Connie turned and saw the light flash fifty yards behind him off the top of the ridge. He hit the edge of the bank dropping toward the tracks and saw the train, a great rolling wall of boxcars twenty yards in front of him. He could see the end of it now, only half a dozen cars still coming on.

"Goddamnit, there he is!" The weight lifter's voice was closer and moving. "He's down by the tracks!"

Connie slid down the bank and ran along the gravel shoulder. The ladder of a boxcar went by him and he switched the briefcase to his left hand. He ran hard, trying to catch it, but the ladder ran faster. He looked behind him. A coupling passed, then the edge of a car. Another ladder gained on him, and he reached out with his right hand, grabbed tight, and jumped. One foot caught a rung, then the other. He held tight, turned, and watched the weight lifter stumbling down the bank, the last car already passing him. Another beam of light flashed off the top of the bank. The two lights glared at him, growing smaller and smaller, then the train wound off into the trees and the lights were gone.

Connie clutched the briefcase and climbed the ladder. When he reached the top, he pushed it across the roof of the car, crawled up after it, and lay down on his stomach. The train seemed to be gaining a little speed now, the rattle and jar of the tracks picking up. He braced his feet against the molding and held tight to the briefcase and the boxcar.

Off to his left, the stones of Riverside Cemetery were sliding past. Then he crossed the interstate, the scattered headlights roving east and west, and saw among the lights of the motels and restaurants on Riverside Drive, the yellow and black sign of the Waffle House. Too bad Rita wasn't working now. He could just jump off here and be gone. But they'd be watching the road for anyone on foot. He knew that. It was better just to ride the train out to the fish camp and pick up his car. An excitement went through him. He was really on his way now. No, they were on their way. He and Rita, on their way to Montana, Plains or Paradise or somewhere in between, on their way to a house surrounded by mountains, to good land and a clear river, and with enough money to get lost for a long time, enough money to start something good, something permanent. He was not like Carl, he had shown them that. And he was not going to be like the old man either. Rita would help him prove it, and they'd prove it in Montana.

Connie thought of the old man and smiled. He liked thinking of him waking up and finding the bills tucked under the lantern. A little surprise for his morning. He liked knowing he'd helped someone, had done something good for a change. Maybe he should have given him a few hundred more. But how long since the old guy had seen even that much money in one place? Maybe never. No, probably never. He'd probably never seen that much money in his whole life. Connie's smile broadened. He hoped the old man would put it to good use.

He did worry about the bums down the track. Would the old man have sense enough to keep his good news to himself? Sure, the old guy was crafty. He'd found himself a good place. And now, with that much cash, he could clean up and get himself some new clothes. Maybe find a room in a board-inghouse where he could get a decent meal, for sure a clean enough hotel room. Anyway, nobody would have to buy him hamburgers for a while. And he wouldn't have to sleep in a grave in the side of a hill.

The train picked up more speed, the wind blowing hard across the roof, brush and the dark arms of trees zipping past at the edge of the tracks. On his right, the yard lights of the Macon Water Works blinked through the trees. He lay his head down on the boxcar and felt the tracks rattle up through the steel and wood. Twenty more minutes and he'd really be on his way. Twenty minutes and he'd be sliding his key into the ignition of the Volkswagen and pulling out for Rita. He thought about what he should say to her when he called, where he should tell her to meet him. What time would that be?

He pulled his watch out of his pocket. It was almost a quarter till four. Make it fifteen more minutes out there and twenty back to Rita's, and he'd be back in town at least by four-thirty. He'd scare her to death, the phone ringing in the middle of the night. But it had to be, he couldn't wait. They needed to put some miles behind them before he called the cops. Yes, that was only fair. And they should probably take her car too. The cops would be looking for his. Yes, they should definitely take hers. The Plymouth was in good shape, and it might be days before the police figured out they were together and started looking for it.

The train moved into the thick darkness of the trees, and Connie thought again of the kid. He closed his eyes and pictured him naked on the mattress. Maybe he should have turned Carl in when he first went out to the lodge with the groceries. He should've told Carl to let the boy go or he'd turn him in to the law. But threats never much affected Carl. Not his threats, anyway. Then there was that way Carl had of throwing the past at him, all he'd sacrificed, all he'd done.

And to see his brother go to jail? At the time it was just too much.

The train was making a slow turn to the left. Connie opened his eyes and pushed up onto his elbows. To his right, he could see the river through the gaps in the trees. It was close now, twenty or thirty yards away, a dull glassy band in the thick darkness of the woods. The wind blew in his face, hard and steady, and made him squint. The train pulled around the long bend and straightened out, veering away from the river, hammering fast through the trees and the darkness. Good darkness now, he thought, the best. The darkness that would open into the good light.

He lay like that for a while, propped on his elbows, the wind making his eyes water. How many times had the old man ridden trains like this? And to how many places? But he wasn't riding it to be like the old man, he was riding it to be different. All he had to do now was pick up Rita. Get to his car, get to a phone, then drive over and pick up Rita. No, he should have her meet him somewhere, the Waffle House maybe, or someplace downtown. But hadn't he already decided that? He took a breath. He was getting tired.

The track shook up through the walls of the boxcar and into his bones. The wind blew hard in his face, and the woods flew by in one long shadow. He didn't know how far he could drive tonight. He needed sleep. But Rita could drive. She was a great driver, and they'd take her car. Sure, they'd ditch the Volkswagen and take the Duster. It was in good shape. It would take them all the way there. And how far was that? Four or five days of driving? Probably, but they could do it in shifts. Rita would have to drive tonight though. He was getting very tired.

The train raced straight on into the woods, and the woods came closer, the black bushy arms of the trees almost brushing the sides of the boxcar. Overhead, the clouds opened up occasionally for a few stars. On his left he saw the gray screen of the old Riverside drive-in, the overgrown yard stubbled with gray posts. He remembered his high school dates there, the agonizing hours in the front seat of Carl's Impala, trying to get a hand up a skirt, a Trojan out of the dash. That's what love was then, the agony of wanting thwarted by the virtue of waiting. There was still something pretty good about that.

The river came close again on the right. Thirty yards, then closer. But the train quickly left it behind, moved on into the darkness of the woods. Then a fear swept through him. What if he couldn't see the lights of the lodge through the trees, or what if the lights were out? What if he missed it in the dark? There were the docks in the river, or what was left of them, but he didn't know if he could see them through the trees. He tried to remember his landmarks. He still had to pass Arkwright, and the lodge was a good way beyond that. The surest thing was the Dames Ferry bridge. If he passed that, he'd gone too far. Maybe a couple of miles too far.

He rode, watching the darkness. The river came back and stayed there, a dull band of glass winding beside the tracks. He watched it flash, disappear in the trees, and flash again. Up ahead a whistle went off and roared back over the train. It went off again, and the trees opened up for a second around a road. He tried to look down it and thought he saw a bridge, but the trees came on too fast. It was probably the River North bridge. That would mean he was almost halfway there.

A light drizzle started to fall. He thought about the money and what he would tell Rita. Where in the world did he come up with that insurance story? Did she really believe that? Probably not, but she wanted to. And that was what was really important. She wanted to believe it. She wanted to believe him. What would he tell her now? What would he say when he called her? How do you explain two hundred thousand dollars and leaving town at four-thirty in the morning? He'd have to figure Carl into it some way. He'd make it gambling money. He'd make Carl look like the bad guy. But he'd already told her the money was legitimate. He'd sworn. Well, he'd just have to tell her he'd lied. He'd lied not to worry her. He'd tell her it was gambling money, that Tommy was mad and they had to get out of town. She'd believe that. She wouldn't like it, but she could live with gambling money.

And she was afraid of Tommy Wilson. If he told her Tommy Wilson was after them, she'd pack in a hurry and go. He knew it. She wouldn't mess around with a thousand questions. She'd pack what she needed and leave the rest.

The rain picked up for half a mile, then suddenly vanished. Over the trees on his right four red lights rose on a tower. He raised his head and watched the lights climb into the sky. It was the tower of the Arkwright Power Plant, four red lights flashing three hundred feet in the sky, four more flashing a hundred feet below them. He rode on and the lights grew larger, then the trees gave way suddenly to a flare of yard lights. The dull yellow windows glowed in the side of the building, the gray steam drifting up into the darkness. The train rushed hard past the coal berm and conveyor belts and dug again into the thick darkness of the woods.

Maybe they should buy another car? Maybe drive to Nashville and trade cars? Or ditch the Plymouth and buy a car outright? Yes, that might be the safest thing. Ditch the Duster somewhere in Nashville and buy a good used car. Something cheap but dependable, so they could pay cash and not look too odd. Maybe even trade again in St. Louis or someplace farther west. It'd be pretty hard to track them then.

The train veered left and around a slight bend, and the river retreated. It was gone for two or three miles of thick woods, then it came back again. He watched it for a while, the glass ribbon flashing dull between the trees, veering away and moving back. Then, far off in the distance, the sky started to lighten just over the tops of the trees. He watched the light widen and grow into a pink blaze. It looked like the afterglow of a bomb, only it didn't flare or die, just hung there, steady and even, the train bringing him into it. The trees broke again, and this time into a bright wash of light, all around him dozens of yard lights on poles scattered through fields of gravel, huge mounds of gravel fifty or sixty feet high, and in front of them the dark outlines of conveyor belts, bull-dozers, and heavy machinery — the Macon rock quarry. The train pushed on through the light, the bright yard dropped back into the trees, and the trees closed to a darkness under the pink afterglow.

He was getting there now, maybe only a couple of miles away, maybe not even that far. He'd have to watch for land-marks — the docks, a light in the window of the lodge. He slid to the edge of the boxcar and looked down at the shoul-der of the track. It flew past in a blur of gravel and brush. How was he going to get off this train? He knew that already. There was only one way off, and that was the same way he'd gotten on. But the train was going a lot faster now.

The river came close again, and up ahead he thought he saw the gray outline of the docks. He eased his left leg over the edge of the roof and found a rung of the ladder. The wind hit him broadside and tried to push him off, but he held to the rail and wrapped himself around the briefcase. He swung his right leg onto the ladder, climbed down easy, and stood on the first rung. He leaned out, looking down again at the blur of the shoulder and the brush beyond it. The tracks quivered up through the ladder, trying to shake him loose. A clearing blew by, no lights, only a gap in the wall of trees and the dull glint of a roof in the darkness behind them. Was that the lodge? He thought for a second. He was puz-zled, the lodge was much bigger than that. Then he knew it was the tin roof of the arbor. He looked down at the shoulder rushing past in a belt of gravel. He didn't want to hit that, he wanted the dark smudge of brush and grass beyond it. He held the ladder and leaned out as far as he could. He let go and jumped.

12

IN THE DARKNESS, the tree frogs barked in high sharp volleys. The wind blew cool and clean off the river and carried the smell of rain. It shook the needles of the pines and combed down the tips of the tall grass. At the foot of the hill the river whispered between its banks, a low rippling over brush and dangling limbs. Only a star or two held out any light, and a sprinkle of rain broke from the clouds.

Connie lay in the grass at the foot of a long bank thick with brush, breathing hard, trying to decide how badly he was hurt. He touched his face. It was scratched and bleeding. So were his hands and arms. His left hand was still wrapped around the handle of the briefcase, but the briefcase was gone. He pushed himself to his knees and looked around. It lay on the gravel shoulder fifteen or twenty yards up the tracks. He stood up and threw the handle into the trees, checked the flashlight in his pocket. Thunder tumbled quietly over the river. He stepped over slowly, picked up the briefcase, and walked back down the tracks. The wind whipped up hard, and the rain blew off to a drizzle.

A hundred yards down, the pines on top of the bank thinned toward the clearing. He tucked the briefcase under his arm, climbed up the bank, and crouched in the narrow wall of trees. There were only two cars parked under the big oak beside the lodge — his Volkswagen and Carl's Cutlass. He crept slowly through the shadows to the edge of the tree line. The upstairs windows of the lodge were black. All the windows were black. He looked down toward the arbor. There was no sign of anyone around, and a strange feeling went through him. Had Tommy moved them someplace? That was just like Tommy. Then the feeling moved toward fear. What was he going to tell the cops? If Carl and the kid weren't here and he didn't know where they were, what was he going to say? Just what he knew, that's all he could tell them.

Thunder rumbled again, faint in the distance beyond the river. Connie stared back at the dark windows of the lodge. No, something didn't feel right. There was somebody else around. He looked into the trees behind him. There was only the darkness and the small noise of the wind in the needles and leaves, but he felt like someone was watching him. He looked one more time across the clearing and down toward the arbor. Only the dull glint of the tin roof and the shadows falling in layers toward the woods. Wind sifted through the trees in a stiff gust and the drizzle stopped. He stepped out of the tree line and walked quickly to the cars.

He crouched behind the fender of the Volkswagen and looked up again at the black window full of jagged glass. Maybe they were up there in the dark. Or maybe they'd left the kid chained to the radiator and beat it. Sure, they could've done that. Maybe something spooked them and they just left the kid up there in the dark. Or maybe Tommy needed to go into town for something. He wouldn't have left Carl, but he could've left the kid. The kid wasn't going anywhere. Then again, they might have taken the kid too. Connie didn't want to go upstairs, but he knew he wouldn't feel right until he was sure. He edged around the back of the Cutlass and walked quietly to the porch. The steps gave with his weight, a slight sag and creak. He waited a few seconds, listening, then crossed the porch and stood in the doorway. The whole house was pitch dark. He touched the flashlight but didn't take it from his pocket, only moved through the door and felt for the banister.

Then he put a foot on the bottom stair and started to climb. Halfway up he heard something. He stopped. The wind slapped a few branches on the roof of the lodge. He climbed to the landing and stood at the end of the banister. Only the wind, the branches against the roof. He walked over to the door, took out the flashlight, and shined it inside. The light found the table, an empty wine bottle, Carl's battery lantern. Then the chair, the mattress under the broken window. The room was empty. They had all taken off. He walked over and stood by the chair. Someone had been drinking Miller. Three cans lay crushed on the table and two on the floor. He shined the flashlight over the linoleum and into the corner by the radiator. It caught the back of a bare leg, hairy and white. Then another leg. Someone was sleeping on the mattress. He moved the beam up and found a smooth pale kneecap. There were two people sleeping, one on top of the other. He caught his breath, swung the flashlight onto the table, found the lantern and switched it on. Carl and the boy were naked on the mattress, Carl's body on top. There was a small blue hole in Carl's right temple, a small blue hole in the boy's left temple, a dark stain on the mattress under their heads.

Connie laid the briefcase and the flashlight on the table and sat down in the chair. He leaned over, held his head between his knees, and breathed through his mouth. So that's what Fry was for. And the whole gang at the graveyard — Tommy had taken care of things already. How long had Carl and the boy been like that? An hour or two? A few hours? Maybe even since he'd left with Mays and the weight lifter to pick up the money. Anyway, it couldn't have been because of him. Forget all their threats. It couldn't have been because he'd run off with the briefcase. He knew that. They wouldn't have had time to get back out here. And there was no phone. No, it wasn't his fault. Tommy had meant to do this all along. He should've guessed that. Tommy wouldn't leave any loose tongues to talk. Not with a kidnapping rap and all that money at stake. He should've known that from the second he'd mentioned Fry. They'd probably planned the same thing for him, in the cemetery, maybe, or on the way back to the lodge.

Connie looked back over at Carl and the boy, the way they lay together on the mattress, their bodies a pale yellow in the lantern light. Whose sick joke was this? Fry's? Tommy's? He thought of Rita, of the way they held each other in the good dark of her room. Yes, the thing to do now was get to Rita. Get to Rita fast and get out of this town. No need to call the police now, just pick up Rita and drive.

He heard a motor. A car in the woods and coming on. He stepped over to the window and crouched. He could hear the roar picking up steadily, then the tires slinging rocks under the car, the fenders hitting brush. Headlights threw a wide tunnel of light into the clearing, then the car skidded in behind them. It was a Monte Carlo. It stopped behind Carl's Cutlass and the headlights went black. Pinyon climbed out of the driver's side, the weight lifter out of the other.

Connie hugged close to the wall. He didn't have time to get back down the stairs. There was nothing to do now but hide, maybe in the hallway, maybe in one of the other rooms. He crawled to the table, picked up the briefcase and flashlight, and moved out into the hallway. In the dim light pushing through the door, he saw a ladder of boards nailed to the far wall. It went up through a hole in the ceiling and into the attic. He walked, easy, over to it, slid the flashlight into his pocket, and started to climb the dusty rungs. Halfway up he heard their footsteps on the porch, light but solid. He climbed up into the darkness, sat on a crossbeam, and slid back against the wall.

Their footsteps came up the stairs, slow. They stopped for

a second at the top, then moved across the landing toward the room where Carl and the boy lay together on the mattress. Connie rested the briefcase in his lap, took the flashlight out of his pocket, and held it with both hands.

"Look at that," Pinyon said, his voice low, almost a whisper. drifting out of the room and across the landing. "Jerry Fry's really fucked up, you know that?"

"Tommy likes him."

"Yeah? Tommy likes some sick shit."

"You don't like it, you tell him."

"Tommy likes some sick shit, that's all."

Connie shined the flashlight across the attic — a few straight-back chairs and a rocker, a stack of broken picture frames, and in the corner to his right, the big tree cradled by the sagging roof. He ran the beam around the jagged boards. Was the hole large enough for him to crawl through?

"How come Fry left this light on?" the weight lifter asked.

There was a silence that seemed to last a long time. Connie worked the beam along the trunk of the tree and back across the attic floor.

"Maybe he didn't," Pinyon said. "Maybe he didn't leave it on. What would he be leaving a light on for?"

"You think that little prick was out here? His VW's still out there."

"I don't know."

"Shit, you think he had time to get out here?"

"I don't know, goddamnit."

The silence again. Then the footsteps moved back onto the landing. They stopped. Connie aimed the light onto the tree and the hole in the roof. He wondered if he'd left prints on the dusty ladder.

"Check downstairs," Pinyon said. "I'll look around up here. And watch out, some of that floor's rotten."

The weight lifter's footsteps pounded down the staircase. The beam of a flashlight — Pinyon's — moved to the ladder, across the bottom rung, and into the corner of the room. Then the light disappeared and Pinyon stepped slowly toward the front of the lodge. Connie wedged the briefcase under his left arm, took his flashlight in his left hand, and stood up carefully under the angled roof. He cut the light onto the crossbeams jutting up from the attic floor. Something banged below him. It banged louder, then scraped off in a high squeal. Pinyon forcing open a door.

Connie shined his flashlight back on the first crossbeam and stepped onto it, balancing himself with his right hand against the roof. The squeal went off again, and he heard a door swing back hard and hit a wall. He stepped to the next crossbeam and worked his way over to the tree. It was a big pine, the trunk splitting open the whole corner of the roof. A few loose boards and shingles were clogging the hole. He reached up, lifted out the shingles, and laid them quietly on the floor of the attic. Another bump — something dropped in the room under him. He paused for a second and listened. Footsteps moved off toward the landing. Then nothing. He reached up again, took the end of a broken board, and pulled it toward him, gently. It made a small splintering noise and came loose in his hand. He bent over and laid the board on top of the shingles. He pulled two more boards loose, laid them down quietly, and climbed out onto the trunk.

There were only a few naked branches near the top of the pine, and the rest of the trunk made a clean slope to the ground. Connie switched off the flashlight and wedged it under his belt. He held the briefcase under his arm and slid down a few feet at a time, backward, his legs wrapped tight around the tree, the bark chipping away under him.

When he hit the ground, he kneeled for a minute in the edge of the woods falling toward the river and stared at the back of the lodge. Nothing moved. He walked along the tree line toward the corner of the lodge and the clearing. When he rounded the corner, he could see the three cars parked in the deep shadows of the oak — the Volkswagen, Carl's Cutlass to the right of it, and Pinyon's Monte Carlo behind the Cutlass. Carl's lantern glowed through the shattered window, but there was no sign of Pinyon or the weight lifter. Connie crept over to the Cutlass and crouched behind the rear fender. The wind moved again off the river, but nothing moved in the lodge. He took out his pocket knife, opened a blade, and pushed it slowly into the tire. The air made a soft hiss as it blew against his hand. He twisted the blade and the hiss grew louder.

When the tire was flat, he crawled over to Pinyon's car. Footsteps moved somewhere in the lodge. He watched the porch, but nothing stirred. He jabbed the knife blade into the front tire — a quiet wheeze. Then the footsteps came again, faint but clear. He jabbed harder and felt the air rush over his hand. A flashlight beam slid through the door of the lodge and jerked across the porch. He twisted the blade and sliced into the tire. The figure of the weight lifter blocked the doorway.

Connie closed the knife quietly and, clutching the briefcase, slid over to his Volkswagen.

The beam of light cut to the cars, crawled over the fenders and through the windows. Connie crouched low beside the Volkswagen, shielding himself behind the Cutlass. He slid the knife into his pocket, dug for his keys, and brought them out. The light shot over toward the woods, then back to the fender of the Cutlass. Connie waited, staying low between the cars. If he opened the door, the weight lifter would hear it for sure. Would he have time to get the key into the ignition, get the car in gear? Maybe, if he waited, the weight lifter would go back into the lodge. He watched the beam of light crawl over the ground at the foot of the oak. The steps moved closer and stopped near the edge of the porch.

Footprints. The ground was hard, but had it rained enough for him to leave footprints? He hadn't noticed any and the clearing was dark. Still, if they were there, the weight lifter would find them with the flashlight. He thought for a second, went through all the steps — jerk open the door, throw in the briefcase, foot on the clutch and key in the ignition, shift to reverse. How long would it take? And what if they started shooting? They would, too. There were two dead bodies upstairs. There was two hundred thousand dollars in that briefcase.

The flashlight beam climbed halfway up the trunk of the oak, then slid back down. It crawled back over to Carl's car, climbed across the hood, and floated through the windows.

More footsteps came through the door and stopped on the porch. "You see something?" Pinyon said.

"Thought I heard something over there by the cars."

"Well, go take a look, shithead. You can't see nothing from here."

Connie heard the weight lifter jump down off the porch, and the panic found him again. He tightened his fist on the door handle, and the fire surged around his knuckles. He tightened the fist again, then changed his mind, let go of the handle. He pushed the briefcase gently under the Cutlass, lay down flat on the ground, and squeezed under after it.

The footsteps came closer, soft in the dirt of the clearing. They stopped behind the Monte Carlo, and the flashlight beam snaked along the ground between the cars, disappeared, and came back. Connie held his breath, his chest wedged tight against the greasy belly of the Cutlass. The weight lifter would see the flat tires, he knew that. And then it was all over. Connie listened, watched the yellow beam jerk behind the Volkswagen and out of sight. He fingered the key ring and felt for his car key.

"Well?" Pinyon said from the porch.

"I don't know. I thought I heard something."

"You didn't hear shit. He's got your head fucked. Check out there around those tables. I'll look down here by the tracks."

The weight lifter walked away toward the far edge of the

clearing. Connie lay still, listening to his footsteps grow faint and disappear. Then he heard Pinyon step off the side of the porch. Pinyon took three steps toward the Cutlass and stopped. He stood for a few seconds, quiet, then walked toward the back of the lodge and into the trees and the brush.

Connie slid a few feet toward the Volkswagen. All he could see were the tires and the clearing peeling off into the darkness. He gripped the briefcase in his right hand and slid out from under the Cutlass. He lay on his back for a second, quiet and listening. Nothing came from the arbor, but the brush crackled steadily behind the lodge. He glanced down at the key ring and checked the key, then got up on one knee and picked up the briefcase. He reached for the door handle of the Volkswagen, popped it, and climbed in. He closed the door easy. Through the rear window he could see the beam of the weight lifter's flashlight darting around the tables under the arbor. He pushed in the clutch and slid the key into the ignition. The Volkswagen turned over and caught.

The light from the arbor swung through his window.

"Shit!" the weight lifter shouted.

Connie hit the gas and the motor revved. He grabbed the stick, pushed down hard, and shifted into reverse. Another light came fast around the corner of the lodge. It caught him with the beam, and he popped the clutch, shot backward across the clearing, turned, and shifted into first.

The weight lifter made a run at him across the clearing, trying to cut him off. Connie floored it, shifted into second, bounced over the dip, and hit the mouth of the road. He flipped the wipers once to clear his windshield, hit the headlights, and shifted again. The brush and the woods blew up around him.

They'd be after him now, he knew that, and he plowed the front wheels up the sides of ruts and pushed on hard, the bottom of the car pounding over the raised center of the road. Dark branches slapped at the windshield and brushed across the roof. They'd be after him, there was no question about that. But they wouldn't catch him, not with a flat tire. The thing to do now was to get to Rita. Get to a phone, call Rita, and get on the road. Don't even go back to the trailer. Leave everything, leave it all, just get to a phone, call Rita, and be gone.

He charged up the road, the tires banging against the fenders. He looked into the rearview mirror. Only the dust turning red in the flare of his taillights and behind it the darkness. But they were after him, he knew that. Even if they had to ride the rim, they'd be after him. He slowed for a turn, geared down, then pushed hard and shifted again. The road opened a little and smoothed out, and he drove harder. Then the pines closed in from both sides, and he had to slow down.

He looked again into the mirror. The red dust and the dark limbs of the trees fading into the larger darkness. But they were back there somewhere, and they were coming. He was sure of it. They'd be coming as fast as they could. But on a rim they wouldn't be able to catch him. On a rim they wouldn't have a chance. Or maybe they'd stopped to change tires? Would they do that? And how long would it take? He should have punctured two tires, a front and a back, two tires on both cars. But then he couldn't have squeezed under the Cutlass. No, it was lucky he didn't do that. He did all right, and it worked out fine. Maybe luck would be on his side for a while. They were coming, Pinyon and the weight lifter, but they'd never catch him.

The road went to a deep rut. Connie geared down and braked, but the front end banged hard. He cut the wheels up the right side of the rut, pushed it, and shifted again. The road smoothed some and he drove hard. Yes, maybe luck would be on his side for a while. He thought about the coin the old man had given him, the eagle with its wings spread out under the stars. That's what he needed right now, wings.

He thought about the old man dropping the coin into his hand, a lucky piece, a memory piece or whatever. Then he imagined the old guy waking up and finding the bills under the lantern. He tried to picture his eyes as he held the bills up to the light. It gave him a good feeling. Maybe the coin was bringing both of them some luck.

In the rearview mirror he saw the darkness closing behind the red dust. He hoped this was going to be the good darkness, the darkness that led to the good light. With just a little more luck he and Rita would see that light together, see it miles away on a highway leading to a good place, Plains or Paradise or somewhere close.

But what should he say to her when he called? And where should he call her from? He'd tell her about Tommy for sure. Tommy would scare her, get her moving. Gambling money, and Tommy was after them? Sure, gambling money, the fights. She wouldn't like it, but she could live with it. And if he said it was gambling money, she'd point most of the blame at Carl. Yes, that was probably the best plan.

He thought about Carl, his white body lying between the legs of the boy, the bullet hole in his right temple, the bullet hole in the boy's left. He remembered Carl's forehead wedged under the kid's chin, the stream of blood running down his face and onto the kid's shoulder, the dark stain on the mattress. He rolled down the window for some air, and a heavy pine scent blew in, filling up the car, calming him some. He'd try not to think about that anymore. What he needed to think about was what lay ahead — the phone call to Rita, the drive to Montana.

When he hit the highway, he took a left and pushed hard over the smooth asphalt. Twenty miles. He'd call her from somewhere on Riverside, maybe the Waffle House. No, not the Waffle House. That might not be smart, he shouldn't go to the Waffle House. He leaned toward the window and caught the clean smell of the pines. The clouds were breaking up over the river, a few stars shining. He was tired and his head and eyes ached. He reached up and felt the cut over his eye. It was crusted with blood and probably needed stitching, but it would heal well enough. So what if it left a scar.

Headlights came up fast behind him. Connie looked into the rearview and saw the lights gaining. He drove harder, leaning through a long curve, but the lights grew larger, brighter, coming on fast. The accelerator was already on the floor, but he kicked down on it with all he had. The lights came right up to the bumper and flooded the inside of the car. A horn blew behind him, a sharp blast, then another. His heart rushed. He tried to push it harder. The horn blew again, a long wail, then the truck came around fast, the wind gust of the trailer blowing the Volkswagen to the edge of the road. He took a breath and let up on the gas, watched the trailer lights shrink into the distance. He was being foolish. They weren't going to catch him. It was all over. The only thing left now was to pick up Rita. Calm down and call Rita, that was the thing to do. Calm down, call Rita, and in a couple of hours they'd be a hundred miles away.

He plunged through another mile of darkness, then in the distance the sky started to lighten over the tops of the trees. It looked almost like a sunrise, and he watched it widen and grow pink, the car bringing him into it. The trees broke open and he shot into a bright wash of yard lights, mounds of gravel, heavy machinery — the quarry again. On his left he saw the tracks and remembered his train ride, the wind in his face, the jar of the steel trying to bounce him off. Already, it seemed like the distant past.

When the darkness closed, he thought again of Carl, his white legs lying between the legs of the boy, the boy's arms handcuffed around Carl's waist. What kind of horrible joke was that? Tommy likes some sick shit, that's all. You don't like it, you tell him. And he wondered which one of them had died first. The boy? Then how did Carl feel in that last second when the shot rang in his ears and the boy went limp under him? Or was it the other way around? Was it Carl who died first? Then what about the boy? What kind of fear was that exactly, the body holding you suddenly becoming only a body? He tried to remember an expression on their faces, but nothing came back to him, nothing that would give it away. The thing to do now was forget about Carl and the kid, there was nothing to do for them. Tommy had taken care of that, or Tommy's man Fry. He'd think about dropping a quarter into a pay phone, about dialing Rita's number and listening to it ring. He'd think about the surprise in her voice and the first thing he'd say. But what would Tommy do with the bodies? Bury them in the woods? Throw them in the river like the hobos had done to the old man's friend? He tried to put it out of his mind. Then he knew what they'd do. They'd just leave them to rot into each other until the cops found them.

He could call the cops, though, tell them where to find the bodies. Tell them about the kidnapping, where to find the boy's mother, Tommy and the others. That's the least he could do. No, it wouldn't do to think about that either. If he called the cops, they'd be after him for sure, and it wouldn't do anybody any real good. They'd probably be after him soon enough anyhow. What he and Rita needed were time and miles. It was enough to have Tommy looking for them. He'd turn the state upside down, maybe two or three states. The cops would be looking soon enough.

Over the trees on his left four lights rose on the Arkwright tower. He watched them winking out their steady red signal. He zipped past the coal berm and conveyor belts, the huge brick building lit with yellow windows. What if they were watching Rita's apartment? What if Pinyon and the weight lifter had gone after him and Mays and Fry after Rita? He imagined them sitting on the benches in the little park across the street. He imagined them looking up through the trees at her balcony and dark windows. It sent a chill through him.

There was only one entrance to the apartment — no way out the back, no way out a window. If they were out there in the park, they'd see her leave, for sure. Maybe it wasn't likely, but it was certainly possible. And possible was more than enough.

He rammed the Volkswagen into the darkness. Ten miles, fifteen, every second worrying about Mays and Fry. Yes, they were out there in the park. He knew it. Maybe not on the benches, but somewhere. Hiding, watching. But they were there. Tommy was too smart not to cover that. Tommy thought of everything. He'd leave no loose ends now. Not with two bodies to cover up, not with two hundred thousand dollars missing.

Then he remembered something. He remembered asking Mays what he'd do with his share of the money. He remembered telling Mays about Rita, and Mays asking her name. Was that all part of his crack about fucking her, or did he really not know her name? Maybe they didn't know anything about her. Sure, it wasn't very likely. Calm down, that was the thing to do. Tommy probably didn't even know about Rita, much less where she lived. Take a breath and calm down. The tough part was over. Get to a phone and call her.

Connie leaned toward the window and let the clean air rush across his face. The clouds were breaking up quickly now, bright stars pulsing in clusters over the trees.

Shit, hadn't Rita said someone was asking questions about him at the Waffle House? Two guys? But that didn't mean they knew anything about her. He hung out a lot at the Waffle House. They could've been asking around at a lot of places — the poolhall, the health club. Just because they showed up at the Waffle House didn't mean anything.

But if they hadn't known about her before, they sure knew about her now. He'd told Mays her name. He'd said it right out loud, my girlfriend is Rita Estes. Stupid, goddamn stupid. All they'd have to do now was look in the phone book and get her address. Goddamn stupid. Would Mays remember something like that? He might. Tommy would for sure, Pinyon would for sure. Mays might. No, he wouldn't. It was such a small thing. Mays would never remember it. Besides, Rita hadn't been in that apartment very long. How long? Two or three months? That address probably wasn't even in the phone book. Relax, the tough part was over.

Connie went around a slight curve, and a long string of lights opened up in the distance at the bottom of the hill — the orange sign of a Gulf station, the blue sign of a Chevron station, yard lights between the blue flags of a Ford dealership. Two or three miles beyond them the boy's mother might still be waiting in her room at Howard Johnson's. The engine sputtered and the car jerked. He shoved in the clutch and revved it. It caught for a second but sputtered again. He looked down at the gas gauge. Empty. A slight fear caught him, but he fought it. The Gulf station wasn't a mile away, and he could coast to it if he had to. The engine sputtered again and went dead. But it was okay now, he could coast to the Gulf station. Everything was going to be fine, the luck was starting to move his way. He could feel it — the solid luck, the end of the bad times, the beginning of the good. He knocked the Volkswagen out of gear and let his foot off the clutch. He coasted down the long hill, thinking about Rita in the car beside him, of the two of them in the Duster now, the two of them driving across the country, the miles disappearing behind them. He took a deep breath and noticed suddenly that he was smiling.

He coasted slowly under the orange Gulf sign and rolled to a stop a few yards short of the pumps. He got out and pushed. A man stuck his head out of the station, but Connie waved him off and pushed the Volkswagen under the awning and up to a pump. He felt really good now, as good as he'd felt in a long time. There was a pay phone on the corner of the lot, he could call her from there. The luck was finally with him, and after all that had happened, he was moving toward a real happiness. No, *they* were moving toward a real happiness, moving toward Montana, toward clear rivers and tall mountains and big sky. He and Rita, moving toward a future, something to build on and something to build with. He filled the tank, hung up the hose, and reached for his wallet. Then he remembered it was empty. He smiled again. That was all right too. He stepped back to the car for the briefcase. Three hours from now they'd be in Tennessee. After that Kentucky, then Missouri, then whatever state lay beyond that one on the way to Montana. Rita could drive while he slept, then he'd take over and let her sleep. In a week, at most, they'd be there, Montana and the big mountains to get lost in. The beginning of something good, something solid. He popped the latches on the briefcase, opened the lid, and stared down at a stack of dirty newspaper. He jerked it out. Under it, more newspaper, torn and dirtied with clay.

13

WHEN HE DROVE under the cream-colored arch of the main gate of Rose Hill and stopped on top of the hill overlooking the valley of graves, the sun didn't appear exactly like a red coin rising through the pines across the river. It was smudged and oblong, but a coin was what he thought of — a cosmic lucky piece radiating fortune and light. It torched the wings of cardinals slicing down the ridge, the red shoulders of a blackbird preening on a terrace fence. It cast a soft pink glaze on the surface of the carriage paths, the damp walls of mausoleums. It blushed the edges of oaks and shaggy cedars, crosses and marble tablets, the concrete walls of terraces tumbling down the hills.

A light shroud of mist was unwrapping itself from the river and the foot of the hills, burning off in the new light rising pink and then gold through the tops of the trees. Church bells rang in the distance behind him, their deep bright notes floating toward the light and the river. He thought of the bell notes riding that light across the balcony and through the window of Rita's room. He thought of her stirring under the clear bright notes of the church bells, of the sun lighting the small hairs on her arms, the five gold rings in her ear. He remembered the way she woke in the morning, how she'd rub her eyes, look at the ceiling, and close them again, and he wondered at the things she saw behind them as she lay quiet in those last few minutes of sleep and half sleep. Maybe this morning, as the bells woke her, she'd remember the plants she used to bring home from church to place in the window of her room, the green plants that meant new life or the flowers that leaned into the sun. Or maybe she'd think of him, imagine them walking through the groves of Tattnall Square Park, the cherry blossoms and azaleas bursting with light, the children dressed in their Sunday clothes, hiding colored eggs in the grass. Or she might just picture them in Montana, a long ride on horseback across their own land — two roans loping through the bitterroot, sheep and burros grazing beside a river winding through a fold of deep green mountains, the sky above them an ocean of blue light.

He took the first carriage path to the left and drove down into the valley toward the obelisk that said PIERCE. He remembered standing there with the old man and looking out over the valley of stones, the old man asking about Rita, if she was anyone special, then telling him of the woman who sang about rivers. Odd how the gray eyes dreaming out of those wrinkles seemed even less a deception now. And then he thought of waiting there with Mays and the weight lifter. He remembered the pistol wedged under Mays's belt, the pistol strapped to the ankle of the weight lifter, the fear that churned in his stomach as he watched the boy's mother walk down the carriage path, the briefcase swinging heavy in her hand. All that seemed like years ago, like something from his childhood, another life entirely.

He could see the obelisk on the ridge now, in the shadow of the oak. It was speckled pink with sunlight. The wind blew across the valley, and the face of the stone rippled with pink blotches. He drove past it and across the ridge above the gorge and the open grave. Light spattered the windshield through the heavy awning of needles and leaves. Sparrows flushed from the grave plots. He parked near the old man's path, picked up the flashlight from the front seat, and got out. The dogwoods on the ridge glowed a brilliant white, their blossoms sprinkled with bees. The sun dropped an orange veil through the oaks beside the road, and he stood for a minute, watching it ripple in the wind coming at him from the river. He walked down the steep hillside covered with brush. The grass in the gorge shone in the new light, a soft green spotted with a silver glaze. The creek sparkled as it washed over bright rocks toward the river. In the far hillside the brick crypts burned pink.

The thicket looked dark and cool, and he didn't want to go in. It was the same darkness he'd felt at the lodge — Carl and the boy lying together on the mattress, their flesh turning yellow in the lantern light, the locked stare of the boy's eyes piercing the air above them, that blank intensity, as though he'd seen something hovering over them, something in that darkness he could never look away from.

A wind stirred the shadows on the ridge, a slight chill. He stepped away from the brush and stood for a moment, letting the sunlight warm his face. And suddenly it seemed as though all he'd ever wanted was light. Long days of it accumulating into years, a fortune of it, a fat wealth he could draw on like a bank account. He and Rita, rich on sunlight, rich on warmth. He thought of it breaking over the balcony and through the window of her apartment. She'd be waking now, rubbing her eyes, kicking the sheet to the foot of the bed. He wanted to watch it spark off the rings in her ear, wash red through her hair as she rolled on the pillow. He wanted to feel its wide shaft warming his legs and chest, to lie quietly beside her and bathe in that wealth.

Across the river a crow cawed, then another, and he watched them drop into the pines. He dreaded going into the thicket — he knew already what he'd find — but he crossed the grass and pushed an opening in the brush. He bent his head under the limbs, crawled in, and let the darkness fall behind him. The flashlight made a thin yellow tunnel, and he pushed on through the brush and the thick shadows of the leaves. It seemed like a heavier darkness now, more a presence than an absence, but he moved through it — ten yards, then twenty, and the wind made a small noise in the treetops. He stopped and listened, and for a second he thought someone might be crawling into the brush behind him. Only the wind. He remembered following the old man into the thicket, then Mays and Fry following him. Goddamn this shit. Go on. Goddamn this shit to hell. Then the pitch dark, the close and stifling dark. He remembered holding his breath at the mouth of the grave, the ball of light climbing a patch of darkness, the noise Mays and Fry made crawling through the brush. It really seemed like years ago, like another life.

The brush thickened, and he had to get down on his hands and knees. He pushed toward the back of the thicket, waving the light like a stick in front of him. The magnolia branches over the mouth of the grave were dark. He shined the flashlight, then crawled toward them. He held his breath, sat very still, and listened for the sound of breathing. The wind in the treetops, the slight rustle of leaves under the shift of his weight. He pulled back the thick branches and shined the flashlight. The grave was empty — the sleeping bag gone, the lantern, the metal box, the paper bags, gone. Only the ragged mattress of old newspaper.

He lifted a foot over the stubs of the bars and crawled in, shined the light across the mattress, scattered the newspaper with his foot. More paper, torn and dirty. His head went light with exhaustion and dread. The old man had left nothing, not even the bills under the lantern. What now? He sat down on the newspaper to catch his breath.

A motor revved and died in the graveyard. He leaned toward the mouth of the grave and listened. A car? On the ridge? Maybe somebody placing flowers on a grave. After all, it was Easter. But this early? He listened, staring across the darkness. Nothing. His imagination playing with the wind. He was exhausted, dazed.

He set the flashlight on the ground and crossed his legs. Nothing? But he'd heard it, the rev and choke, the motor shuttering down. Somebody placing flowers on a grave? Sure, it was Easter. Somebody placing lilies on a grave. By noon the whole cemetery would be covered with them. He propped his elbows on his knees, lowered his head. The old man hadn't left a thing. And where was the old bum now? Alseep in some boxcar on the way to Atlanta.

A noise again, far off in the thicket — a quiet breaking of sticks. He listened. Only the wind. An animal, a bird. They hadn't had time to follow him. They were still on the highway halfway back to the lodge. Or were they? How long could it really take to change that tire? Then the snap again, distant but clear, and a slight panic made him dizzy. He lay down on the mattress and braced against it. Carefully, he reached over and switched off the flashlight.

The darkness closed around him like a room circling a drunk.